Travel broadens the mind, so Jonny had heard. And even though it wasn't his mind he was thinking of broadening, a job as a travel courier seemed an ideal way to get to grips with people – preferably the female variety.

Rupert Colt wasn't the best employer – his six-shooter wasn't exactly straight – but Colt's Travel Agency was as good a place as any to start a new career.

And so Jonny found that not all Russians believe in the Cold War. Some like it hot.

And Swiss misses can turn into hits.

In Amsterdam he made an exhibition of himself.

And Paris in the Spring had plenty of bounce.

Jonathan May's latest adventure proves wilder and funnier than ever!

Confessions of a Travel Courier

JONATHAN MAY

SPHERE BOOKS LIMITED
30/32 Gray's Inn Road, London WC1X 8JL

First published in Great Britain by Sphere Books Ltd 1975
Copyright © Jonathan May 1975

This is for Jane H — the lone rearranger

TRADE
MARK

Set in Intertype Times

Printed in Great Britain by
Hazell Watson & Viney Ltd
Aylesbury, Bucks

ISBN 0 7221 9330 0

CONTENTS

Chapter Nine

Paris in the spring is a disappointment. The only things that Jonny gets there are things he could well do without. A go-go dancer turns out to have some great surprises for him. More suspicions are aroused.

Chapter Ten

Friday the thirteenth is indeed unlucky for some. Jonathan May says farewell to one old friend and meets another in the most surprising surroundings. He makes a splash to remove all those nasty suspicions. Dark though things look, our hero is not downhearted and we leave him looking brightly to the future.

CHAPTER ONE

Hello.

I said, 'Hello'.

All right. Be like that. Carry on sitting there with your lips as tight as a Liverpool defence.

I mean, I'm only trying to be friendly. Sort of, set the tone for the book. Still, I'm not one to push water uphill. If at first you don't succeed, try again. Then give up. No point in making an idiot of yourself.

Old readers will know that I'm Jonathan May. Others will have to find out for themselves. Hello, new readers, wherever you are!

Remember when I stopped at Stoppers? The departmental store in hard day's Knightsbridge? I spend the best year of my life there, and finish up with little to show, except some very odd experiences. (Author's Note: All this has been detailed in the previous bestselling title in this series: *Confessions of a Shop Assistant*, also by yours truly.)

Now, I accept that some of you might not yet have had the pleasure. Sorry, I'll write that again. Some of you might not yet have read this wonderful book. 'I laughed and laughed' – Bernard Shulman. 'Will have them rolling in the aisles' – Milton Walker. 'I have never read anything like it' – Malcolm Muggeredge.

N.B. That's Malcolm Muggeredge with an 'e'. Not Malcolm Muggeridge with an 'i'. Heaven forfend!! No, this bloke Malcolm Muggeredge is someone I meet in the 'Flog and Nightgown' a month or so ago. He says he's read *Confessions of a Shop Assistant* and he tells me he's never read anything like it. He adds several other compliments that modesty forbids me repeating.

Actually, I escape him only by clambering through the window of the crapper. Funny man, who I suspect is a little more than somewhat unbalanced. I mean, he suggests that

7

I don't write these books and they're all figleafs of my imagination.

Anyone would have to have a sick mind to think this was actually fiction. Who could ever make it all up?

Where was I? No, love. Not climbing out the window of the crapper. That was before.

I remember. I'm telling you about the end of my last magnum opus. That's a sort of gun, like Clint Eastwood carries. Very big and powerful. Long and strong. Dynamic.

His gun's not bad either!

Look, tell you what. I'll save a bit of time and just tell you the last bit again. Imagine the sorrowful scene. Out of work, feeling as much use as a spare pike at an angler's wedding. Walking through the bustling streets of colourful Soho. Avoiding the colourful meths drinkers and the colourful pools of vomit. Past the colourful clippers with their colourful dialogue.

In films, the scene goes all shimmery and we are in for a flashback. Oh, dear. Tell her someone that it doesn't mean a new way of exposing yourself! Thank you.

We can't make books go all shimmery, so use your imagination. Back. Back. You are going to sleep. No! Just relax. Don't get so tense. By the axolotl! I sound like Nicholas Parsons in 'Sale Of The Century'.

Here we go.

Back.

Back.

'I fancy boldly going where no man has gone before. I'm after new horizons. Open air. Force myself into something new, or does that sound like virgin on the ridiculous?

'Wait a minute! What did that sign in that window say? The travel bureau? There; it says: "Courier wanted. Experience not essential."

'In I go. There's a dazzling blonde sitting behind a desk, thumbing through some brochures. If that blouse was any tighter, she'd need paint stripper to get it off.

'I walk up to her. Her eyes light up with a wave of apathy.

' "Yes?"

' "I'm May." '

' "You may what?"

Right. Now we all know what's going on. Who I am. What I'm doing and where I am. I can finally start.

(Publisher's Note: About time too.)

(Author's Note: Belt up smartipants. Know what a publisher is? He's the grit in the vaseline of literature.)

I look pityingly down at this poor frail little flower. Ten stone if she's an inch.

'My name's May. Jonathan May.'

She takes a deep breath, and I swear I can hear the cotton moaning under the buttons. 'Great. What do you want? A medal?'

I lean on the edge of the desk in my best Paul Newman manner, ready to charm her with my easy grace. Sadly, there are more leaflets on the edge of the desk, and my hand slips. Like the latest trade figures, I plunge floorwards, bringing half the brochures with me.

Over the canned music disposer Stavros Givusakis and his Bethnal Green Bambinos carried on plucking the guts out of 'Long-haired Lover from Liverpool'. I have never heard a worse load of silly pluckers!

I lie there, rubbing a badly bruised pride, waiting for the lovely lady to assist me to my feet. Instead she assists me with her delicate size six, straight up the Khyber.

'Clumsy great twit,' she snarls, as charming as a were-wolf under a full moon.

Discarding showers of heliotrope books and pamphlets and brochures, feeling as though I've been smothered in bright yellow sand and bright blue sea and sky, I stand up.

'Pick 'em up then.'

Normally I would take pleasure in telling such a maiden exactly where she can insert each of those hand-outs, but I fancy the job, so I bend humbly down and replace them on her desk.

It's an excuse to flash a glance at her legs, which look just about my thighs. Apart from a small ladder in her tights, which just beckons me to climb it, they are not far short of perfect. Smooth, firm, tapering up to a scrap of white at the very, very, very, very, very top.

Pause for deep breathing exercises.

'See anything down there you fancy?' she says, as delicately as a drag-line excavator crushing a row of houses.

I wonder whether the job is worth this sort of insult. I ponder on the chances of saying 'I've seen better legs on a pub piano'.

I don't say it.

Instead, I mutter something that she takes as an apology for my fearsome lust. She smiles, showing a fine set of choppers. I wouldn't mind getting cheek to cheek with her. Gnashers to gnashers – lust to lust!

Finally, the status quo is restored. I see a sign on her desk giving her name. Mary Krissmuss. A nice bit of Danish pastry.

Mary, Mary, how does your status quo?

'Pardon me . . .'

'What's the matter? You farted or something?'

Now, I have to say that there is one thing about women, up with which I will not put. That is coarseness. I don't mind a dirty joke here and there. Or there. But the otherwise lovable Miss Krissmuss has done herself in the Jonathan May stakes. She is a non-starter. She doesn't even come under starter's orders.

Her loss, folks.

I put on my executive look, which involves tilting up the end of the nose and raising the voice as though one's braces are too tight.

'I'm interested in the vacancy advertised in your window. Is it still open?'

There will be readers among those present who will spot this one coming. Just pass further along the page, please.

Bleeding clevercuts!

Mary looks vacantly at the vacancy sign. 'Is it open?' she asks like a badly taught parrot.

'Tut, tut,' I say, regretting I'm not yet old enough to get

away with a scathing 'Hrumph!!!'. 'Open those lumps of gristle you jokingly refer to as ears, and listen. I said, "Is it open?" and that's what I mean.'

'Course not. Too bloody cold at this time of year. Only a loony'd open a window when it's February. I mean, you'd have to be pretty thick to open a . . .'

'Not the window!' I say calmly, my voice splintering glass at fifty paces. 'The sign on the window!!! Is the job still going?'

Miss Krissmuss at last realises what I'm on about, and promptly loses any interest. She begins to excavate something unpleasant from her nose with a stained Dirtex.

'YeahinthereandspeaktoRupert.'

'Thanksalotandmayyourelasticneverwither,' I retort with the famous May charm, and walk smartly towards a door marked 'Private. Knock and Enter'.

I do both.

A little voice flutes out a glad cry of welcome. In I go.

My hand is clasped in a grasp like ten pennorth of frozen hake, and I get a whiff of something like my old man brought home as a trophy of his time in a Turkish brothel while liberating the East and making the world a better place for the Americans to exploit.

'Hello. Hello. Hello.'

Can it be Dick Emery doing his honky-tonk bit?

Bleeding nearly.

I'll start at the bottom.

As you were.

I'll start at the top.

A wig. To say just that is like saying the Mona Lisa is just a picture.

This wig is curly and bleached and tinted and too big for his head. While he's shaking my hand with all the vigour of a princess in a leper colony, the wig's flapping up and down like a gooseberry in a lift.

Soft, pink little face with those giveaway puckers by the ears and along the jaw that mean face-lift. This guy hasn't just had a face-lift. He's had a full overhaul and refit.

Blue eyes, like ice in suet pudding. Mouth with the finest

11

set of teeth any dentist was ever proud to call his own.

Lilac cravat. Purple shirt. Burgundy jacket. Violet trousers with an indiscreet check. Mauve silk socks and dark lilac shoes. He's like a character out of a kid's cartoon.

Beware of the 'Purple Pumpernickel'!

'Hello,' I say, enthusiastically, trying to get my hand back. I don't know what to do first with my fingers. Count them or wipe them.

'I'm Rupert Colt. I'm a straight-shooter, if you know what I mean. Where can I whisk you to?'

'What?' I ask, feeling like a spare rick at a haymaker's wedding.

He walks to a huge globe in the corner of his . . . No. Sorry. Used the wrong word there. Not 'walks'.

Try again.

He minces to a huge globe in the corner of the room and sets it rotating with a casual flick of his limp index finger. I suss out that he may be about to come over with a gay day. I should worry. As long as it's not me he comes over.

He stabs at the globe, hitting India right up its sub-continent. 'How about San Francisco?' He breaks, and that *is* the right word, into a swift chorus of 'I Left My Aunt In San Francisco' or whatever it's called.

'No? How about exotic Mandalay?' His finger – with pale violet varnish on – hovers over Melbourne. Rupert strikes a pose and . . . not a po dear. This isn't about torture chambers. Strikes a pose and declaims in a mock-heroic way 'Come ye back ye British soldier, come ye back to Mandalay'. His cheeks go all pink at the thought.

'No. You see, I'm only here for . . .'

'Tangier?'

'No, listen to me. Hear what I say.'

Hands up those who recognised a line from a Buddy Holly song. For those who didn't, well, I guess it doesn't matter anymore.

He stops like someone's goosed him with the flying fickle finger of fate. All the pinkness runs way down off his plump cheeks, and his jaw sags like my old man's stomach after eighteen pints.

'You're not . . . you're not . . . you're not from the police?'

That last word comes out like it was something you don't say in polite company. Before I can answer, he starts to jabber on with all the words pushing each other out of his mouth so fast that some of them fall on their faces.

'If it's about that boy scout then I can sexplain. I mean, I like boy scouts. No, I don't. That's not what I mean. I mean that I was just showing him some unusual knots and I came over all queer.'

Beads of sweat sprinkle his shiny desk.

I manage to get a word in. 'Look, Mr Colt. I'm not from the police.'

'Honestly?'

'Honestly.'

'Cross your heart.'

'And hope to die,' I say solemnly.

'So you do want to go on a trip?'

'No. I've just come about the job.'

'Aah.' Brisk efficiency replaces meandering vagueness. He straightens his cravat with hands that shake and shiver and quake and quiver. 'Who sent you in?'

I point back to the outer office. 'The young lady there.'

'Mary Krissmuss?'

'And a Happy New Year,' I say, not to be outdone in the politeness stakes, though it is a bit late for such Yuletide cheer.

He eyes me up and down like I've come in a gift-wrapped parcel marked 'Rubbish'.

'I see. Well, what's your name?'

This time I'm careful in my phrasing. 'My name's May. Jonathan May.'

A little grin slinks up out of the mud and plasters itself on Rupert's face. 'Bet you get lots of jokes about May what. Don't you?'

At this point I reckon the time has come to cut my losses and stroll gently on to the local Labour. But I'm thinking of giving up the flat in Longlea Road, and some of the crackly folding greens would not come in unhelpful. I swallow my pride. 'Pride – the tablets for humble men. As used by Uriah Heep. Swallow one when humility is desired.'

'Sometimes, Mr Colt.'

'Call me "Rupert"; there's a good boy. We're a friendly ship here. All equal.'

I have heard this load of old fertiliser before. I'm sure you have, too. The boss who says that is the one who expects you in at nine on the dot while he swans in about eleven. Then, after a twenty-five-quid nosh with some other old drunk at a highbrow eaterie, he staggers off home at four. Rings you from his home at five-thirty, just to make sure you're still there.

Bosses! Most of them, as my old mum back home in Birmingham would say, would go twice round the pan and are pointed at both ends.

I worked for a bloke once, and he went home in a collapsed state just because his electric pencil-sharpener wasn't working properly! Said he couldn't face another day of roughing it.

Back to Rupert Colt.

'I get some teasing from some of my friends about my name.'

'They call you Rupert Bear,' I say, determined to show myself bright and keen.

I see right off that I've boobed again. His face goes all pink, clashing horribly with his purple outfit.

'No! Certainly not! I'm known as "Quick-draw Colt". You see it's a play on my name. Colt was a gun. And . . .'

I laugh, naturally. Only, it sounds to me like the wail of a hyena across the eternal sands of the Sahara. No, I've never actually heard that, but it's what I *imagine* it would sound like.

At last, just when I think my legs are going to drop off, he waves me to a seat. One of those cane-bottomed things that leave marks all over your trousers. I sit down, and he lights up a cigarette. I don't smoke, but it would have been nice to have been offered one.

From behind a cloud of stinking smoke that reminds me of the time my old man burned my old mum's rubber corset on a bonfire, Rupert tells me all. About the job.

The office is nice and warm, and I'm wearing my winter woollies. Life has been a little up and down – if you know what I mean – over the last few months, and I'm feeling about as alert as a fly in November. Rupert's words wash over me like warm honey, bathing me in a sea of travel agent's platitudes.

Gradually, I slip away from the present, lulled by a vision of life as a travel courier. Sun-swept sands, golden and unspoiled. Palm trees with the fresh Caribbean wind rustling through their nuts. And I can tell you that you have not begun to live until you've had a warm wind blowing round your nuts.

Dark-skinned alohas that beckon to the shy lua with their proud, firm, jutting wahines. Well, something like that.

Rupert can sure sell an image. He tells me of the wonderful life of the travel courier. Parties of rich American nymphomaniacs eager to put out their all under the summer sky of Rome/Naples/Paris/Amsterdam/Trinidad/San Francisco/Tokyo/Singapore/Hong Kong.

Masked balls in Hong Kong. Hong Kong. Hong Kong ...

'Are you listening to me, Mr May?'

The sharp little voice pierces straight through my lovely dream world. I sit up briskly, stifling a yawn.

'Of course I am, Mr Colt. Er, Rupert. You were talking about holding King Kong's balls.'

A puzzled expression crosses my brow. Was that really what he'd been talking about?

No.

'Mr May. Jonathan. I was talking about balls in Hong Kong with my American matriarchs' tour number four. Please try and pay attention.'

I mumble my apologies and sit up. He goes on.

And on.

And on.

You know the sort of interview I mean. Where the guy goes on forever about what a great firm his is and how lucky you are to have the chance to sweat your life away working for him.

Still, as I've said, Rupert sells it well. I can hardly wait to head for the sun and wallow in the pleasures of warm and willing flesh. I should tell you that I have not done a deal of said wallowing for some time.

'Well?'

By the Blessed Oliver Plunkett! I've done it again. Dozed away in mid-stream. The May brain is often an organ resembling a soggy sponge. But, when up against it, it can resemble a first-grade computer. I exercise it, desperately groping for something to say that will show my eagerness. I knew a bloke – my old uncle Angus, in fact, who would slumber through all manner of meetings. When prodded, he would sit up and say brightly: 'I can only agree with everything that the last speaker said.'

Finished up Managing Director he did.

Poor devil!

'Fine!'

Rupert beams. I've done it right at last.

'Well, then, when would you like to start?'

'You mean, you're offering me the job?'

Rupert's face darkens. 'Of course. That's what I've been talking about. Eleven hundred pounds and all the tips you get.'

When actually pushed to the brink of employment, nervous tension always strikes at me. After Stoppers though, I reckon I can put up with anything. The thought of all that spare on coach parties to Dubrovnik, not to mention Hong Kong, drives caution to the back row of my mind.

Only one thought makes me pause. 'But, Rupert. You know nothing about me.'

He smiles. If they remake 'A Tale of Two Cities', he's a cert for the bloke who operates the guillotine. 'I go a lot by instinct. If I like someone, Jonathan, then I really like them.'

He stands up and walks round his desk. I shrink in my chair and cross my legs. 'You'll start tomorrow. No, give you time to get out of those silly old casual clothes and buy something smart to start in. Let's say Monday.'

'Monday,' I say dutifully. The vision of warm sun and sea drives me on.

A hot little hand rests on my shoulder, the fingers squeezing gently at my quivering flesh. 'There. I think that we're going to be really good friends. Don't you, Jonny? You don't mind me calling you "Jonny", do you?'

'No,' I squeak, wondering whether to try and get up or stay where I am. The insult to my best bit of gents' suiting has dug deep. My uncle Chris who runs 'Smartique – Clothes For The Discriminating Male' in Smethwick would be struck to the core of his flinty heart if he heard his imitation mohair being so slandered.

'We'll have a gay time together, Jonny.'

'I'm sure, Rupert.'

Not while I have muscles in my legs we won't.

His hand on my shoulder is weighing me down. I drop my left side, giving a fleeting impression of the Hunchback of Notre Dame. 'What's put your back up, Quasimodo?' Ho, ho, ho.

He's now leaning so hard that his hand falls off my shoulder and he nearly goes base over apex to his torn lino. The smile slips off for a moment. So does his wig, but he hurriedly puts both back in place.

'Did you hear the one about the gay cowboy, Jonathan?'

Actually I heard that about the same time as I used to toddle round the playground of Sundial Lane Infants chanting on with: 'On top of Old Smoky, where nobody goes, there sits Betty Grable without any clothes. Along comes Roy Rogers, going clickety-click. He leaps from the saddle and . . .' I'm sure you don't want me to go on.

(Publisher's Note: We certainly don't!)

But I believe in giving the boss what he wants. Well, I do draw the line at certain things. So I smile with all the conviction of President Nixon. 'No. No, Rupert, I haven't heard the one about the gay cowboy.'

'He rode into town and shot up the sheriff.'

Muffled gurgles and splutterings reveal that Rupert is not one to leave his own jokes unlaughed at. He collapses pinkly in his swivel executive chair, wheezing like my Grandpa bending down to pick up the empties.

I smile pleasantly. 'Very funny, Rupert. I like that.'

He wipes his brow with a pale lilac handkerchief. Gradually his breathing returns to normal. 'Good, good. We'll see you on Monday then. Unless you're free for a nibble of something later this evening? No? Ah, well. Perhaps when we've got to know each other a bit better.'

I stand up to go.

'One thing, Jonny. I expect loyalty from my employees. I shall want you to back me up at every opportunity.'

Max Miller at the Alhambra, Manchester, second house on Saturday couldn't have given that line more meaning. I decide to cool the scene down a bit with a calming exit line. As I close the office door, I say enthusiastically: 'Don't worry, Rupert. You can rely on me to bend over backwards for you.'

Mary Krissmuss sniffs: 'Not another one!'

I decide to go to the pictures. I walk into the first cinema I come to. It would be 'The Odd Couple' they're showing!

I go back to the flat.

There's a brightly-coloured postcard waiting for me in my rack. From Kingston, Jamaica. It says: 'Brotherly and sisterly love from Morrie and Melanie. Having a lovely time. Wish you were here.'

I can imagine the laughter and sniggers when they write that bit. The very idea of poor, honest brother Jonny ever getting anywhere there's a bit of sun and sin! Little do they know. I look forward for the first time to seeing the faces of my brother and sister as I roll up at their hotel in the West Indies. Yes, this job is going to be a winner.

Somehow my room doesn't seem so bleak. Rupert has laid a pile of brochures on me, and I scatter them carelessly across the bed in a splash of superlatives.

Where will my first task be? Rupert mentioned a short period of training under one of his more experienced executives. I could even put away my prejudices and work under Miss Krissmuss. The thought sets springs running through my loins.

I reach under the mattress for my well-thumbed copy of

Men Only. Relax with the certain knowledge of a day well spent.

I imagine myself on a hot beach with the long-legged, centre-spread, Rosemary, whose hobbies I learn are 'pottery and folk-singing. She just wants to be happy'.

Don't we all!

CHAPTER TWO

The date is Monday, 10 February. Devoted readers of the last epic tome (this tome wasn't built in a day either) will know that I livened up the leaden dullness of *Confessions of a Shop Assistant* with snippets of information as to famous people who had birthdays on special days in the book.

Not this time. I mean, it'd get boring, wouldn't it? And it takes me a lot of time to check them out. Anyway, you don't like them, do you? If you do, then I'll carry on with them. Because this show is for you and only. The clapometer is just for fun. Enough to make Hughie green with envy!

You do? Honestly? All right then. Larry Adler. The one who played the theme from 'Genevieve' all the way from London to Brighton and back on his gob-iron. Harold Macmillan. The good fairy who ran the land of 'You've never had it so good', when a lot of us had never even had it at all. And Jimmy Durante. Schnozzle! I must admit that I could never see that Durante had any kind of talent at all. I mean, Robin Day makes me laugh more.

The previous week has passed all too fast. I am now the proud possessor of a new suit, bought with my last week's salary from Stoppers. I go up Stoke Newington to a little bloke someone once recommended. Al Albert – 'personal attention at all times'. He looks like a well-worn pair of socks himself, but he is a fantastic tailor. I tell him it's urgent, and he gets anxious. 'I can't normally make a two-piece suit in under twenty-four hours, Mr May.'

I gulp. I explain that in a hurry means five days, and he relaxes. 'No trouble. Come for your fitting tomorrow.'

I do. Very nifty. When I say I bought it with my last cheque from Stoppers, I should have made it clear that the suit cost more than I earned in a month. But I think of all those fat tips – nearly put a 't' instead of a 'p' there – and I pay up with an approximation of a smile.

It seems to be time to move on from Longlea Road. Too many cherished memories there. But that might have to wait until I have some more of the ready.

It's raining. It's pouring. The sky has that leaden consistency that I always associate with my mum's Yorkshire Pudding. The water soaks through my Smartimac, nestling coyly down my neck, inside my shirt. At nine o'clock I'm outside the door of Number Eight (A) Newman's Court in Soho. The rain hasn't washed away the evidence of a massive technicolor yawn in the doorway.

To pass the time I eye up some of the tempting offers in the window of Colt's Travel Bureau. 'Colt's 45 Holiday Ideas!' I count them. Well, there isn't anything else to do. There are 31. 'Colt's Colossal Cornucopia of Circumambulatory Holidays.'

Listen, smiley, if you can think of a word beginning with 'C' that means holiday, then don't tell me. Tell Rupert Colt.

Dead in the middle of the window, just above the smear of . . . whatever it is . . . is the poster that covers all my fantasies. 'Twenty-eight days in sunny Barbados.' That's the one. Luxury beyond the imaginings of man. First-class travel and accommodation. Experienced couriers to cater to your every whim. I know a few whims I wouldn't mind catering for. Edgar is getting so little exercise these days (and nights) that I look at him each morning for signs of deterioration. Can't be good for the little (modesty) chap.

Also, he doesn't like cold, wet weather. Shrinks right away to himself. One rather twee young lady of my past acquaintance once took things in hand, yittering on about how it was like a 'lovely rosebud, so soft and tender and innocent'. Which is more than she was!

But on this freezing day, almost deafened by the clanging of brass monkeys, I can tell you that the darling buds of May are not at their bubbling best.

Nine-thirty comes and goes. I've done the Quizword in the *Mirror*. Laughed three times at the same Hector Breeze cartoon. Wondered if Garth and Astra will ever find true happiness.

Wondered if I'm likely to die of pneumonia before I start my job. The way things are going, I hope Rupert doesn't decide he wants to see my testimonials. I'd have to defrost them first.

Surely someone must come soon. If not, they'll find me frozen to the doorpost like some loyal sentinel. What a load of cobblers! How stupid to stand there until you freeze to death. I'll give them just three more minutes, then I'm going to exit stage left with great rapidity and that Rupert Colt can take his miserable job and stuff it right up his . . . 'Good morning, Rupert. Lovely for the time of year.'

He looks at me with an expression on his face like my old man when he put his dentures in one morning and found a couple of earwigs had shacked up in them.

'What do you want?' he asks, his voice as warm as the inside of a deep freeze.

'I'm May.'

Are you sitting comfortably? Get your head down in the dugout. It's coming over. The joke you love to hate. A big hand for it. Here it comes; the 'May, what?' gag.

Rupert looks up at me, his fingers fumbling in his pockets for what I hope are just his keys. Either that, or he's practising for a challenge match in the pocket billiards tournament.

I repeat. 'I'm May.'

'May what?' says Rupert tetchily. At last he finds the key and the door creaks open.

'Rupert. I'm Jonathan May, and you've hired me and I'm here to start today.'

'Of course you are,' he mutters, glancing through his mail absently. I notice a brightly-coloured card from some sunny clime in the mountains. A regular hill clime.

He switches on the light and the cockroaches scurry for cover. There is no sign of Miss Krissmuss, which is something about which I have mixed feelings. Ladies like her I can take or leave. Or sometimes take *and* leave. Her desk is as clean and bare as a vegetarian slaughterhouse.

Gradually, memory comes back to Rupert and the joviality seeps through his Monday morning surliness. He even favours me with a smile, and waves me vaguely to a spare desk in the corner of the office. I'm not saying that the desk is old. All I'm saying is that there's a small notice pasted inside the top drawer. It says: 'In case of attack by Zeppelin!' I won't tell you the rest; it's just a load of hot air.

I sit down, only to leap to my feet at his master's voice, calling for me to slip out and bring in two coffees and a hot sausage French.

'What's happened to Miss Krissmuss?' I ask, sussing out that I'm landed with the unclean end of the stick and am liable to end up as super-office-boy.

'Miss Krissmuss's wrist had a cyst. She missed an important list and we were dished. Though I wished she'd fish it out.' I regret not wearing my raincoat in the office as that sentence proves rather a wet experience. And you can spray that again!

'I have not yet replaced her with a permanent secretary. We will manage with a temp.'

She wanders in at eleven, hews three letters from the living Tipp-Ex, and then vanishes never to be seen again. Not that she is a great loss.

I seem to spend the whole day bringing an endless supply of hot sausage French's from Levy's salt-beef store across the courtyard. This is not really an establishment that deserves any publicity. If my mum could see the standards of hygiene, she'd throw up . . . her hands in disgust. And she's no paragon. You can eat your dinner off her kitchen floor. In fact, it often tastes as though you have.

Somehow, Rupert never quite has the time to tell yours truly just what he's supposed to be doing. Finally, as the afternoon darkens on in towards evening, I beard him in his den.

Figure of speech, love. It means that I stride in and bang on his desk and say: 'Er, pardon me for interrupting you, Rupert . . .'

His face matches his suit – a light pink, reminiscent of the sort of socks Teddy Boys used to wear. Course you remember Teddy Boys. They were like greasers with style and string ties. Rupert goes for the all-in effect in colour. So, if

23

his suit is pink, then so are all his accessories. He even has a collection of wigs in matching shades. Rupert makes David Bowie look like Cliff Richard when it comes to gear.

The reason for his pink face is the magazine that he's been furtively studying and which he's tried to slip furtively into his drawers. His drawers are obviously full of other things, and the magazine flops to the floor.

Helpful Jonathan bends down and picks it up, unable to resist a quick glance at the cover. It shows three well-greased young men admiring each other's, well, you know . . . admiring each other's . . . Words fail me here, and so does my nerve. I notice that two of them are nice Jewish boys, when Rupert snatches it from me.

Incidentally, it was called 'The Wellie Boys'. Danish. Load of rubbish I reckon. I can see a better developed body any time I saunter by a mirror.

'What do you want, Jonny? You can see I'm busy.'

Being busy like that will bring him nothing but hairs in the palms of his hot little hands. I think that, but I don't say it. I remind him in the nicest way that I signed on board as a travel courier and when do I start travelling.

'Soon. Very soon. Of course. Last year the number of bookings abroad was down a bit, but there's still lots of openings.'

I bet there are, and I bet he knows them all.

'You said one of your regular couriers would help me out. Take me in hand.'

He beams so hard that I fear for his health. 'I could always take you in hand myself, Jonny.'

'No. No thank you, Rupert. I'm sure you've got your hands full as it is.'

'Well, things are slack.'

He can say that again. We've had three wrong numbers and eleven kids in who want to do a project on Singapore and can we give them some handouts. I give them a swift handout round the back of the head, and that's it for the day. Not even a caller for a wet Thursday at the rhubarb thrashing at Saint Bueno's.

Finally, Rupert admits that he hoped I'd help out in the

office. I suggest with my maximum tact that in that case he can bid me a fond farewell. Rupert admits that he could do with another courier, as he's just lost two in unfortunate circumstances. I press him for details, but he clams up and changes the subject. Since I'm more interested in me than in what happened to my predecessors, I let it pass.

'Very well, Jonny, my sweet boy. Tomorrow I will arrange for some girl to do the office chores and you shall go out with one of my ladies to see the sights of London as you've never seen them before. Leonora Laide will be your tutor.'

I like the sound of the name. It has a ring to it that has a promise. Will it be kept? Patience. All – nearly all – will be revealed.

I thank Rupert and he seems happy. I'm about to leave when he looks up. 'Jonny, dear heart. Did I ever tell you the one about the gay Baron?'

I grit my teeth and force out a negative reply. As long as you only say something like 'Yes' or 'No' then teeth-gritting is all right. Anything longer and you sound like a ventriloquist with a strangulated uvula.

'Well, this gay Baron. He had a funny hobby. He loved to go serf-riding.'

Boo-boom!

It is time to go flat-hunting. I am so up to the whatsits with Southern Region that I consider the heady pastures of North London. That evening I have a quick nibble in a bistro in Dean Street and set off to the great untracked wastes of Camden Town and Caledonian Road. All I know about this far north is that they have wolves round the doors in winter.

It's cold enough for snow at the moment. A hot-dog seller is bawling his wares (a dachshund does the opposite. If you get it, explain it to your friends. A joke shared is a joke doubled, I always say) on the corner of Dean Street and Old Compton Street.

Just as I'm walking past him, there's the faint hiss of something whirling through the air, and a rotten egg spreads itself across the man's shoulders like a stinking cloak. The man, seemingly a native of the sunny island of Malta from his language, is very angry and capers up and down, screaming and cursing.

I only mention this true anecdote as an illustration of the way to make a Greek urn. Sorry, Venetian blind. Bugger it! A Maltese cross. That's it.

I wish I hadn't bothered.

The evening isn't wasted. I've got a local paper and ring round three or four places first. One of them sounds a possible. Within spitting distance of Holloway Prison – remind me not to walk to windward of the jail – and in a quiet cul-de-sac. Bacon Hill.

The landlady's daughter opens the door with a smile as big as all outdoors and glasses as thick as yesterday's cream.

How do I know she's the landlady's daughter? I've read this joke before, haven't I? Silly question.

The front door, painted in a bilious shade of brown – the sort of colour that mothers with young babies know so well – edges open and this happy face peers out. Not bad looking if it wasn't for the cheaters. Edgar perks up for the first time in many a long day.

And night.

'I'm Jonathan May, and I've come about the flat.'

The door opens a full millimetre more. 'Hello. I'm only the landlady's daughter but . . .'

The rest is lost in the howling of a dog. Now I know quite a lot of the 'She was only the ————'s daughter, but she . . .' jokes. You know? You don't know? Then pin back your ears and get ready for a couple of samples. Which reminds me of yet another joke about a specimen. It goes like this . . .

(Publisher's Note: Sorry, readers. We felt it was a bit too strong. The joke, not the specimen. And we decided not to pass it. The joke. If you'd read it like we did, you'd have been grateful to us for cutting it out.)

Well, I bet you liked that one. Didn't you? Not too near the knuckle, was it? Right, now here's the others.

She was only a colonel's daughter, but she knew what Reggie meant.

26

She was only a gravedigger's daughter, but she loved to lie under the sod.

And, last but not least: she was only a fishmonger's daughter, but she knew how to lie on the slab and say fillet.

There are lots more, and I'm sure there must be one about a landlady's daughter. If you know one, please send it to me at the publisher's. I can always steal it. Oh, what a giveaway! I mean use it.

Back to Holloway. The young lady invites me in to have a look round, explaining that her parents live out in the country but she lives on the premises and looks after things. She apologises for her state of attire. A loosely-wrapped towel that reveals some intriguing hillocks and mounds. Not at all a flat attire!

Her name is Linda Loveband, and she has a smashing deep-throated voice. She makes me a hideous cup of not very instant coffee and shows me the flat. Two rooms and a kitchen with a back garden the size of a table-cloth.

We sit on the sofa. Chatting of this and that, but in the sort of way that reveals that we are both thinking of the other. I agree terms for the flat, and promise to move in by the weekend. All I have is a suitcase of tatty clobber, another case of books. My precious sound system, and my even more precious records.

'I'll look forward to having you, Mr May,' says Linda with a wicked smile.

'I'm sure I'm going to reciprocate,' says I.

I fear that lovely Linda is not of the brightest. She looks worriedly at me and says: 'In that case, shouldn't you go in the loo. I've got some tablets for upset tummies.'

I explain that reciprocate means . . . well, I bet you know. She smiles. 'Would you like a little nibble, Mr May?'

'Don't mind if I do, and the name's Jonny, Linda.'

The nibble turns out to be some rather crumbly shortbread. Now mammy's little baby may like shortnin' bread, but I can't stand it. Like eating the dust out of an Egyptian mummy's belly-button. I make a manful effort, sprinkling myself with crumbs.

Linda brings in a cloth, still clad, of course, in her towel,

27

and wipes me down with a deal of energy. Since most of the crumbs are on and around the battle area, my old red-nosed burglar thinks he's heard the call to short-arms and raises his head. Linda blushes and rubs on.

When she straightens up, the corner of the towel has somehow got hooked round one of my jacket buttons. An amazing and unlikely coincidence! I heard someone say that. They haven't tried digging a small hole in a strong bath-towel and manipulating that hole over an adjacent button in twenty seconds flat without the wearer of the towel knowing what's going on.

'Ooooooo!' she goes. Surprisingly quietly, I think. A good omen. Her right hand tries to cover up two of the most splendiferous breasts I have ever gone cross-eyed over. I say that she tries, because you'd have to have a pair of hands like Morgyn the Mighty to cover up those two free-thinking beauties.

Her left hand waves vaguely in the vicinity of the passion chasm, seeming anxious not to disarrange a single hair. I sit still, disentangling the towel from my person. I think that Junoesque is the word to describe the charms of Miss Loveband.

'Well, are you just going to sit there and look at me all evening?'

No red-blooded Englishman could refuse such a challenge. Nor can I. I stand up, and remove the right hand and then the left hand from their feeble attempts at concealment. My arms go round her – just – and I take off the glasses. I have always wanted to do that bit where the fellow takes off the bird's glasses and she's revealed as a raving beauty.

I would like to be able to say that Linda fulfils my ambition. She merely looks like a nice girl who's lost her glasses.

Ah, well!

She pulls me towards her, her right hand now busy doing a smashing job in liberating Edgar from his confines. Eager to show off his paces after so many weeks, he can't wait to get on with the action. Neither can Linda, and she's on her back on the bed in the corner of the room with Edgar making a better acquaintanceship with her interior fittings before you can say 'How Dutch is that moggy in the window?'

Certain things rise and fall and other things go in and out and it all comes off rather well. Both Linda and I succeed in climbing every mountain, if not exactly at the same moment. Still, I reassure her, there's plenty of time to practise. And practice, as we all know, makes for mutual satisfaction.

I pull up the strides and she wraps up. In the towel again. Feeling a little sticky here and there, I give her a goodbye kiss, to seal the deal on the flat, and go on my way rejoicing.

Somewhere to live and something to do during the long winter evenings both in the same day. And there's lots more to look forward to tomorrow when the job gets moving. I can't wait to get on the job. Sorry. On *with* the job.

I walk through the freezing blackness to that Mecca of light and cleanliness, Caledonian Road Tube Station. As usual, the lifts are either not working or stuck permanently in the outer darkness at the bottom of their well, so I brave the winding staircase and catch a train southwards.

Get off at Leicester Square and walk down Charing Cross Road ready to go home to Hither Green. The post-cinema crowd are wending their way homewards as well, and the train is fairly crowded.

I sit opposite a youngish couple. The guy is built like a flabby lamp-post, with a beard that would have been better strangled at birth. He talks with all the energy and conviction of the true bore and his girl looks as though she's about to fall asleep.

Quite a pretty little thing. I tell a lie. Actually, she has a rotten complexion, bad teeth and greasy hair. Her contribution to the conversation is largely grunts.

But the fellow keeps pressing her to make some decision. I think it's something about where they're going to go. His place or hers.

He keeps on and on at her. 'What do you want? Just tell me and we'll do it. How about coffee at my place and then back to yours for the rest of the evening?'

No answer. Her pale face is sunk in her coat collar and her grunts get softer and softer.

29

His voice has all the charm of a hacksaw blade drawn down a sheet of metal. I'm just wondering whether to belt him one or get out and change carriages, when the gods intervene.

He says: 'Come on, Tracy. Buck up and tell me what you want. Come on.'

She sits up and turns to face him, showing the first signs of life. 'All right, Roger,' she says, 'I'll tell you what I want. I want to be bloody sick.'

And she is.

When I get back to Longlea Road, there's something else to cheer me up. A letter from Elizabeth James – readers of *Confessions of a Shop Assistant* will recall her as an unhappy married lady with a nice line in nice lines. When I say she's an unhappy married lady, I mean that she's happy but her marriage isn't.

Actually, that isn't true either. The letter is very happy because she's not married any longer.

And she's thinking of coming down to London. That would bring even more light into my life. Liz has this trick with her . . . no, it would be ungentlemanly to reveal it. Anyway, I want to keep it to myself.

There's a little joke in her letter, and I slip into the arms of sleep still grinning at it. As you're still with me after all these pages, I will share it with you.

Couple of men riding a tandem round and round a block of flats. Fourth time round, a dog comes out and throws a bucket of water over them.

Get it?

Got it?

Good.

Night.

30

CHAPTER THREE

Apart from King Farouk of Egypt – the fat one with the greatest collection of porn the world has ever known – 11 February is somewhat devoid of famous people. What a thing to be remembered for. Overweight and oversexed.

It is with that sad thought that I wake up in my room in Longlea Road, contemplating the pleasant idea that I have only four more nights to go. Then it's me for the North. I know Holloway is hardly Orkney and Shetland, but it's north of Hither Green.

The morning is as black as a baboon's basement.

I break the ice on the washbasin and plunge my face in for a refreshing wash. The toothbrush handle catches me a sharp one up the left nostril and I begin to wonder whether this is going to be one of those days best spent huddled up in bed in the pre-natal position with the blankets piled high.

Baked beans on toast hardly make the morning sparkle. They may mean Heinz to a million housewives, but they don't tickle my rise-and-shine palate. I glance through the paper while breakfast settles leadenly in the pit of my stomach. There is also a cup of coffee swilling around down there plus my morning dose of Brek-Break. 'The laxative for those who can't even pass the time away. Gives your bowels that wide-awake tingle.'

I could not say, go the bowels of Jon May.

I put on my new suit. I hate wearing a coat, whatever the weather. Don't really know why. Suppressed virility thing, I expect. Rush out of the front door, dodging a whine from the landlady, and a claw at my strides from one of her damnable cats. She – the landlady, not the cat – seems worried that I'm about to do a moonlight on her.

The very idea. May I be struck dead by lightning on the spot if such a thought was true. Yes, I suppose I did move sideways a bit sharpish then.

Round the corner and up the slope to the station. It's

been freezing hard during the night and the hill is as slippery as the inside of a pie-dish. In front of me a very pregnant lady topples over and slides down on her stomach, helpless as an overturned tortoise. The bowler and brollie brigade watch her with the incurious gaze they reserve for any human happening that they don't want to get involved in.

Gallant knight that I am, I rush to help her and set her on her feet. Make sure the baby's not on the way. Get her ticket for her. Assist her back up the slope.

And miss my bleeding train ! ! ! ! ! !

Still, I reckon that the office probably won't open till ten, like yesterday, so I'm not worried. There's a limit to the number of ways that Sod's Law can operate.

Wrong. Rupert is there fuming at the mouth. Or, should that be foaming? Maybe both. In the . . . what?

You've never heard of Sod's Law! You're joking! How many times have you stood at a bus stop and watched them all going the other way? That's Sod's Law. Drop your slice of bread and jam. Which side hits the floor? The jammy side. Sod's Law.

Get to the station five seconds early, and the train's half an hour late. Get there five seconds late, and the train's on time. Sod's Law. Never fails.

You see, on Monday I was there on time, and everyone's late. Today I'm a bit late and Rupert's right on the dot. In every way.

Spotted suit, shirt, tie, hankie, shoes – whoops; not his shoes. He's just walked through some mud and got splashed.

'Well, well, if it's not Jonny. Nice of you to come in. How wonderful of you to actually honour us with your presence. I can recall the search parties. Let the news agencies spread the word to a mourning world. All is well. Jonny is found. The prodigal has returned.'

I am genuinely impressed with his flow of sarcasm, unmatched except by a great eccentric who taught me at Birmingham. His nickname was 'Coco' and he wore a deaf-aid. Nobody was ever sure really whether he was joking or not.

One thing's for sure. Rupert's not joking. A pale-faced girl sits cowering behind her typewriter, trying to look busy

32

and avoid catching the master's eye. I see no sign of Miss Laide. Perhaps she's got mislaid!

When I ask Rupert, he explodes. It's quite funny, because he isn't the tallest man in the world. He's the only keyhole peeper in the world who has to take a stepladder with him everywhere.

'Leonora Laide!! I'm going to fire her! The moment she appears! She is f-i-n-i-s-h-e-d. You!' at the timorous temp, nearly making her wet her winter knickers. 'Get me Leonora Laide on the phone.'

She gazes blankly at him.

'Get me Laide on the phone!!'

Apart from a small windmilling movement of the ends of her ten beautiful fingers, there is no sign of action. Rupert goes to pull his hair out by the roots, but remembers just in time that he hasn't got any. No, his wig isn't spotted today, apart from a nasty stain where some careless pigeon's done a whoopsie on him.

'I want to get Laide!!!!!!!!' It is a cry from the heart that rings round the small office like my Uncle Bert when he's a bit over-emotional and thinks he can sing like Caruso. He's not bad on quantity of sound, but the quality is lacking. His wife can't keep goldfish because he keeps cracking the bowls with his bellowing.

'I want to get Laide !!!!!!!!'

'Don't we all, dearie,' says a quiet voice from the back office.

Three pairs of eyes swing round to stare at the newcomer. The temp sniffs and goes back to cleaning her typewriter with a nail-file. Rupert looks on the verge of an apoplectic fit. For a moment I think I can see steam rising from under his wig, but I decide it's a trick of the light.

This is obviously Leonora Laide. Blonde hair, rolled up in a tight sort of curl at the back of her head. Green eyes, slanted like a cat's. Difficult to make out much of the body, as she's wearing a fur and leather coat that conceals most of the contours. But there's enough still showing to make it an interesting thought that I'll be working under her. Her ensemble is completed by dark tights and black thigh-length boots.

'I warned you about this! Time and again.' Rupert's voice cracks into an even higher register when he's cross. He waves his arms around and jumps up and down. The last time I saw such an exhibition was on a picnic when a wasp got inside my mum's directoire knickers. Now there's a word I don't get to use much nowadays. No, twit. 'Directoire', not 'knickers'.

Leonora props herself casually on the edge of my desk, favouring me with the sort of friendly, relaxed smile she'd give if she'd found she'd walked in doggy droppings. I wilt. So does Edgar.

'Rupert. Don't be such a tiresome little poof.'

There is a tiny tinkle in the corner. The temp has dropped a pin she was using on her machine. It sounds like Big Ben. I hold my breath and try to remember my first aid for cases of heart seizure.

Rupert twitches, and his face goes white. I really expect him to hit her. Or faint. Or rise vertically into the air. He does none of these things. Just opens and shuts his mouth several times, not unlike one of my Uncle Bert's late-lamented goldfish.

'Now, now, Rupert. Would you want our lord and master to know everything? About your little sideline in imported periodicals? Or, about that nasty business on your Superstuds' Tour of seventy-four in Athens? Wrong bedroom, wasn't that your excuse?'

'Now, now, now. Let's have no more of this sort of talk, Leonora. One big happy family. Eh?'

'All right, Rupert. Anything you say. You're the boss.'

There's something in the way she talks that puts the fear of God in me. As it obviously does in poor Rupert. What can she mean by 'our lord and master'? And who is the real boss? The plot begins to thicken.

My musings are interrupted. They are not amusing musings. Rupert is introducing me as 'the newest member of our happy company'.

A cool hand is extended. I shake it. Leonora would not be

fun at Indian wrestling. I retrieve what's left of my fingers on the off-chance I might want to use some of them again.

'I'm pleased to see you.' I stammer.

'I can see you are,' replies the charming Miss Laide, not even bothering to look at me.

But she does look at me when Rupert, somewhat recovered, informs her that I'm the new courier, and that she's taking me with her in fifteen minutes on the London Tour with thirty-eight American tourists from Des Moines, Iowa.

Leonora eyes me up and down, as though she is judging best of breed at Crufts. I fear that I fall short of whatever her standards are, but Rupert is inflexible and we walk off together towards our picking-up point at Cambridge Circus. Both of us wear badges that proclaim: 'Colts for Class'.

Actually, we don't quite walk together. It's more like an Indian husband and wife, with me playing the wife and trailing along three yards behind, trying to dodge the puddles. Every now and again she throws a crumb of conversation over her shoulder. Kind, reassuring words.

Like: 'I wish I knew what I'd done to God to make him saddle me with a clueless berk like you.' Only 'berk' is not the word she uses.

Suddenly, she stops, and I bump into her, nearly knocking her over. 'Wait a minute. Your name's Jonathan May?'

'Yes.' I mean to say, I could hardly deny it. Though I have been known to at odd times.

She laughs, showing the finest set of choppers this side of the Horse of the Year Show. 'That explains it.'

You're wondering what she means, aren't you? That is, if you haven't fallen asleep. So am I. Wondering, not falling asleep!

But, despite all my pressing, she won't come across with any more information, and clams up tighter than my old man when Winston Churchill's mentioned – he reckons he should have had the job. But, every now and again, she gives a hoarse laugh. Not a horse laugh, a hoarse laugh. On second thoughts, she gives a horse laugh. More of a whinney – not as in Churchill.

Just round the corner from Cambridge Circus, she stops

again, and again I bump into her. 'We can't go on meeting like this,' I quip merrily.

I once saw a horror film where this bird who'd washed her snakes and couldn't do a thing with them kept looking at men, and they all froze on the spot. Solid stone. She was called the Gorgon. I remember her reading a French novel by a writer called Emile Zola.

Right load of old cheese it all was – this Gorgon's Zola!

I'll pause a moment here in this thrill-packed narrative while you wipe the tears of merriment from your mincies at that last jest.

Feeling better? Then I'll go on.

The freezing look is what I get from Leonora. She ignores my attempt at familiarity. But she does at least speak to me. She says: 'Step on my heels once more, sonny, and I'll separate you from your marriage prospects.'

The thought obviously pleases her, and she becomes more friendly. You know, like cleaning your teeth before you spit in someone's face. That sort of friendly.

I peer round the corner and get an attack of stage fright. Or, should that be coach fright? There's a huge gleaming coach that says on its side: 'Shuckburgh Transport – We Never Miss A Trick'. Sadly, some naughty fellow has slightly adjusted one of the letters in the last word, which rather spoils the effect.

Alongside it is a collection of American tourists. There should be a collective noun for that. Like a flock of sheep. I've got an old book that gives masses of those names. Would a brief educational digression not be in order? Amaze your friends with this useless information.

How about a shrewdness of apes? Or a gam of whales? Or a crash of rhinoceroses? Or an exultation of larks? Or what about a . . . (Publisher's Note: This goes on for about three pages so we've cut it out. We knew you wouldn't be interested. At Mr May's personal request, we've allowed him one more.)

Right. A misery of publishers. Yah boo to you.

But what about American tourists? A drone? No, too

quiet. More like a bray. Better. Yes, that's it. A bray of American tourists.

The men loaded down with check jackets and cameras with multiple lenses. The women in blue rinses, plastic macs and striped pants. All braying away at each other.

'Thirty per cent widowers. Fifty per cent widows and the rest miserably married,' hisses my tutor.

'Listen,' I hiss back, heartened by the fact that she actually spoke to me. 'I don't know the first thing about London. What do I do?'

'Watch me. I know less than you, so I make it up as I go along. Throw in a few old stories and collect the tip at the end. I'll start, and you can carry on.'

Carry on to disaster, the last thing in a long line of British comedies. All it needs is Charles Hawtrey playing Cedric Softwinkle!

'But where are we actually . . .?' The chill wind from Charing Cross Road blows my question back in my face. I am alone. Miss Laide has gone to meet her little flock. Sorry, little bray.

They see her badge and home in on her like a flock of Mid-Western vultures. Questions pour at her, but she ignores them and climbs on board the coach, leaving them muttering sullenly on the pavement. It's beginning to rain. Long cold fingers that smear themselves over my face, racing for the warmth under my collar.

Reluctantly, I clamber on board after the last of the Americans. Leonora is tapping the microphone in a professional manner. As I climb aboard I can't help noticing that the casual way she sits exposes an exciting amount of thigh, up above the boots.

And then some!

She waves me to sit by her. As she half-turns in her seat to face the eager throng, her breasts press against me. All at once I think we may become bosom friends after all.

'Hello, and welcome to Colt's London package. Sorry the weather is so awful but I'm sure we'll have a jolly super time together. I'm Leonora and this is Jonathan. Why don't we all say "Hello" to each other.' There is a chorus of

37

croaks from behind me. I grin at the absurdity of it all, when a sharp elbow nearly knocks Edgar off his perch. I stifle a squawk, while Leonora whispers savagely, maintaining her fixed smile: 'Say "Hello" to them, you dumb bastard!'

Appalled by her ferocity, I do my best.

'Let me just quickly read out a few conditions before we start.'

At breakneck speed Miss Laide rips through a set of rules and regulations that would keep a good Chancery lawyer in work for years. I catch snippets of it.

'The company additionally, without any prior notification and without any guarantee of remuneration, claims the right to alter the terms and conditions of the hiring. Colt's Tours, in conjunction with Shuckburgh Transport, further reserve the right to alter at any time the route, price, hotel or itinerary owing to any circumstances whatsoever and not withstanding. It also reserves the right to cancel the running of any holiday, tour or coach due to insufficient customers. Or for any reason.'

There's a lot more. You can guess how fast Leonora reads it all. The coach pulls away from Cambridge Circus just as she starts. By the time we pass Old Compton Street, she's finished.

Note: For those not cognisant of the purlieus of London, the distance between Cambridge Circus and Old Compton Street is about fifty yards.

It all passes over the heads of the tourists, who are busy fixing their array of cameras and checking light meters. One or two of the women look bemused, as though they're suffering from some sort of culture shock. Leonora keeps them happy with a stream of information about the buildings they pass.

Potted guidebook stuff. 'Foyles – greatest bookshop in Europe.' 'Centre Point – tallest white elephant in the history of the world.' 'Fleet street – home of the newspaper industry.'

And so on and so forth. Such simple stuff that I reckon even I could handle it. We reach Saint Paul's Cathedral, and

Leonora gives me my chance. She splits the party up into two halves, and lets me have one lot.

The amount of knowledge I have about St. Paul's could be easily written on a dwarf's jock-strap. But I recall Miss Laide's words and decide to bluff.

As I shepherd my dazed throng among loads of other dazed throngs – it's never too early for the tourist, nor the weather too cold or wet – I beat them about the ears with a mass of information.

One eye wanders to my watch, for the magic time of eleven eighteen when the coach leaves for the Tower of London. I have trouble with one elderly Des Moinian, suffering from some respiratory disease. He lags behind, and we have to keep waiting for him. But he's heard about the Whispering Gallery, and is determined to hear it.

We get up there, with my stock of myth and fable about the Fire of London, Sir Christopher Wren and the Blitz rapidly running out. Bliss; time is also running out. After the Whispering Gallery it'll be back to the coach and another quick rub up Leonora's chest.

Did I tell you that we seemed to be getting closer? I didn't? What an oversight. Every time she turns to address her party, she presses harder against my chest with her . . . her chest. Once, ever so casual, her hand drops into my lap and gives Edgar a quick once-over. He gets all excited and waits for the once-in and out.

Meanwhile, back in the Whispering Gallery. I arrange my little gaggle in a row round the walls, like all the others. Then I tell them to whisper and listen.

A deal of breathy Iowa hissing and clucking. The gentleman with asthma drops his false teeth with a resounding clatter and we all have to start again. Clear as crystal, we hear words floating back to us out of the ether.

Ether as in air, not as in anaesthetic.

But the words are not those that began to wing their way round the second largest church dome in the world. Yes, I'm surprised by that, too. And, no, I don't know which is the biggest. I guess it's probably in Rome. I do know though that the biggest dome anywhere is in Texas, at the Houston

39

Astrodome. The reason I know this is that I have been told it fourteen times already by an old goat with a camera lens so big that he must be trying to prove something.

Back to the whisper.

'No! Stop it, Antony. Antony . . . Ooooh, you cheeky . . .' Muffled groans and grunts, with a few squeaks for luck. Most of my Americans are looking shocked, though the asthma sufferer looks as though he's having the best time for years. I wonder whether to cut my losses and leave.

'Antony, get your hand off . . . No, you'll tear them . . . Antony! Oooooh, Antony, someone might come.'

At last, we hear Antony. 'Me.'

Giggle, giggle, giggle.

The clicking of official heels ends the whispering rather abruptly. I gather my tattered flock about me and we rush for the coach. Leonora already has her lot on board, comparing postcards.

By the time we get to the Tower, it's starting to snow. Leonora hustles everyone out through the main archway, and we stop by the souvenir shop. I am amazed to see how many tourists there are. I have not yet heard of the off-peak half-price bargain-buy.

'Listen, everyone. Jonny and I will escort you to the Crown Jewels, and from then on in you're on your own. I'd like you all back here by twenty-past twelve. Any questions?'

A well-corseted matron with more wrinkles than a plate of tripe raises her hand. 'Will we be able to see the little Princes, miss?'

Leonora favours her with the look that chills. 'No. That is myth. We are not concerned with fairy stories. Are we?' In an aside, she mutters: 'Not like our dear boss, eh?'

I find her arm through mine as we walk up the wide flight of steps by the White Tower. I've been here once before with a school party when I was about thirteen. Can't remember much about it. Just the thrill of saying over and over 'Bloody Tower. Bloody Tower! *Bloody* Tower! !'

A shrivelled harridan grasps me by the other arm, her lacquered claws tearing my shortie overcoat. As an overcoat it would make a good sponge. Rain goes through it and the wind whistles round my own set of jewels.

'Yes?' I say tersely.

'I wanna know why those boys are not dressed properly. Tell me that?'

I look around for the local flashers, but can see nobody dressed improperly. God knows, it would take a brave and dedicated exposer to risk frostbite in his favourite member on a day like this. All I see are a couple of sombre-suited Yeoman Warders.

'Where?'

'That Beefeater. He should be a resplendent sight in his picturesque crimson and gold uniform. Why's he wearing that dull blue?'

The May wits are sharpened by the keen wind. 'Because today's 11 February. Anniversary of the death of William the Conqueror, builder of the Tower of London. If you'd come any other day but today you'd have seen them in their proper gear.'

She toddles happily off to pass this dishonest gem of wrong information on to her crochet cronies. Leonora stops and smiles at me. 'You know, Jonny, that wasn't half bad. You might just make it after all.'

I hope I can make it – but not quite in the way she means.

The queue for the Crown Jewels stretches twice round the backside of nowhere and then snakes back again. Leonora groans. 'Wait a minute, I'll go in and see what I can do.'

Two minutes later she returns and we jump the queue, to the delight of our party and the obvious irritation of the other poor folk freezing to death outside.

As the warm glow of the gold envelops me in well-being, I ask her how she managed the miracle.

'Easy. Told the warder in charge that I had a party of Americans from the International Sufferers from Dysentery and I couldn't answer for the consequences if they were kept waiting.'

Which reminds me of another nice joke, but after what the Publisher did last time, I don't think I'll bother.

There's the usual braying and chattering at the relics of

England's past. It must have been all right in those days, having salt out of those great golden jerries. They like the actual jewels and 'Ooh' and 'Aaaah' like everyone else. Me included.

Then it's a quick canter across the courtyard, glancing at the ravens as we go. A less raving lot of ravens I have yet to see.

By Norrokin and Borrokin, but it is hellishly cold!

Our Americans slip into the hands of one of the professional guides – the warders – and we suss that we can safely leave them to it, with a quick reminder of when we're meeting again.

As we tiptoe away, the warder is just saying: 'And here, on the spot marked by this plaque, fell many a flower of England.'

'I'm not surprised,' croaks our asthmatic friend. 'Damn near tripped over it myself.'

Into the White Tower, which I reckon would split up nicely into a few luxury flats. The day will come. Whenever I see this sort of place, all the old red blood of the Mays comes to the fore, and I start looking for the nearest lamppost.

Oh, Gawd! To hang people from, of course. What do you think I am, a bleeding dog?

Incidentally, my Uncle Angus, that I've mentioned before, was a well-known agitator back home in Brum. I say 'was' because he suffered a rather sad end. He always claimed he was a red-hot Communist, though he spent most of his life angling for the foreman's job, so I doubt his integrity. The foundry where he worked was all out, and he decided he'd sleep in one of the big furnaces, so that they couldn't use them. Trouble was, he got Brahms and Liszt and forgot to tell anyone what he was doing.

The dispute was settled that day and work started again. It wasn't until someone asked who was cooking hamburgers that they found him. No, it didn't kill him. He's the sort of bloke who'd walk into the local flower shop and come out smelling of sewage. He was just a bit scorched round the edges, that was all.

Spent the rest of his life on Social Security, claiming he got nervous if he even thought of work. I don't mind work. In fact, if I had the chance, I could happily watch blokes working all the live-long day.

The Beefeater on the door gives me the look he obviously reserves for snotty-nosed children and hippies. The edges of his waxed moustache positively bristle at the sight of me, but he gives Leonora a smart salute and a bright smile.

As I go past, I whisper, 'You've got a run in your stockings, mate' and he stops smiling like someone's rammed a halberd up his Traitor's Gate.

The place is more or less deserted. A few children drooping along behind earnest parents, and a couple of blank-looking Czechs.

We browse among the suits of armour, admiring the stamina of those old knights who carried all that iron around with them. It can't have been easy. As well as wearing one of those uncomfortable chastity belts all day and night.

What do you mean? Don't be ridiculous! As if a woman would ever be persuaded to wear one of those things. I mean, it'd be a bit unhygienic, wouldn't it?'

The weather is worsening.

Reminds me of this knight who's lost in the forest, and his horse has fallen and broken its neck. He comes across this lonely castle, where the Lord breeds giant dogs. About eight feet high. Uses them for riding and hunting. The weather's appalling but he doesn't want this strange knight staying, because he's got three lovely daughters. All virgins. So he insists. Offering the knight one of his special pets to leave on. Then his eldest daughter stops him, saying: 'No, father. Surely you wouldn't send a knight out on a dog like this.'

Inside the Tower, it's as dark as a camel's cavity. You can hear the wind whistling round the corners of the building, and up through the cracks of the floor-boards. I shiver and Leonora looks concerned.

'What's the matter, Jonny? Are you cold?'

This is like asking a witch, burning at the stake, whether she's too hot. I smile bravely and shake my head. Chips of ice tinkle from my ears.

'Never mind, love. Come with Leonora. I'll warm you up a bit. There's one place I know. Along here.'

We are so close together that Edgar is nearly beside himself with excitement at the prospect of action. I do believe I am about to get Laide.

Through dusty corridors, along to the Chapel of Saint John. When I see the sign, I pull back. There are things at which I draw the line, and humping in church is one of them. But she reassures me with a squeeze that sends the blood pounding.

We go into the crypt, and she pushes the door quietly to behind us. 'There. Now we're all alone and we can get on with things.'

I look round the gloom and nearly have kittens on the spot. All round the walls are chains and manacles, with thumbscrews and racks and irons and . . .

'It's a torture chamber!' I squeak. Going back to striking a pose, and torture chambers a few dozen pages ago, a torture chamber there is, of course, a po with spikes round the top.

'I don't go in for all that strict discipline and bondage stuff,' I say wildly, trying to get her arm off mine.

'Silly boy,' she says, patting me on the shoulder with her left hand. Her right hand is on one of those liberating exercises and her lips are getting closer and closer and clo . . . It's rude of me to talk with my mouth full.

She leads me by what decency insists I call the hand to a small cell just off the crypt.

'This is where Walter Raleigh was imprisoned,' she tells me cheeringly. 'It's very small and private.'

There's hardly room to swing a cat. But there is a stone shelf that is just about big enough for our purposes. Having crept into the crypt, I want to cuddle and creep out again.

Despite the weather, Leonora peels off layer after layer of clothes. If you're the sort of reader who gets bored reading a description of a lovely lady taking off all her clothes, then I don't know what you're doing with this book. Go away and get stuck into 'A Thousand And One Things A Bright Boy Can Make From A Loofah'.

44

Go on, sling your hook.

Right, now for those lechers left . . .

While she's standing up, I take off her coat and lay it on the bed. Stone is such a chilling prospect to one's prospects, I always think. A tight jumper slips over her head, despite getting hooked up on her chesty protuberances, which are very protuberant. A pale gold silk blouse unbuttons down the front revealing a steamy amount of pink flesh.

'Are you still cold, Jonny?' she whispers, her tongue playing a toccata in my ear.

'No,' I stammer, through a mouthful of shoulder. My fingers are trembling so much with lust that I can hardly manage the buttons. This may be the lust time, I don't know!

After the blouse, I have to reach right the way round her to unhook the half-cup bra – 42C if you're interested. Hey, what are you doing still here? Get back to your loofah!

She's such a big girl that I have to force myself to stretch and get the bra off, feeling as though someone's poking me in the chest with two sharp fingers.

While I'm doing this she's got my coat and shirt off, and is working at my zip. My meat-machine is getting ready to lift off the launching pad.

Leonora sits down and I unzip her boots. This means I have to kneel down and hold her by the thighs to lever them off. This is a surprisingly sexual activity and I can recommend it as a starter. She wriggles her bottom up and down and the tights slip off easily. Her bare feet tickle my fancy before she stands up so that I can get her skirt off.

I'll recap the situation here. I'm in my smart purple pants, having removed all else while on the floor. Leonora is a splendid figure in pink knickers with white lace round the tops.

Somehow we don't seem to be feeling the cold. Just each other.

Right, you can come back from your loofah now!

She whispers loving things in my ear as we sink to the fur-covered bed. The door is closed safely, and we begin to get to know each other better.

I feel sure Sir Walter wouldn't have minded.

Edgar is trying to loop the loop, enjoying the feeling of being caught in a warm, wet vacuum-cleaner. At times like this I tend not to notice anything going on around me. As with the Princess in Stoppers' Fairy Grotto, you may remember.

Leonora is driving me on like Lester Piggott, using heels and hands, and is keeping up a running commentary in a rising voice. I wouldn't notice if a Beefeater opened the door.

A Beefeater opens the door.

No, he doesn't really. I haven't quite finished yet, and neither has Leonora. We'll slip outside into the crypt to see if there really is a Beefeater there. Let's pretend there is. What sort of things do you think he'd be saying?

'In this tiny cell, Sir Walter Raleigh spent the last tragic months of his last imprisonment. To combat the intense chill he would strip, to the buff, if you'll pardon the expression, ladies, and exercise for hours on end.'

Right. Leonora and I are *just* completing our business to our mutual satisfaction. Just ten more. Eight. Six. Five. Four. Three.

It is at *this* moment that the door is thrown noisily back. I'm not going to chuck it all away, and neither is Miss Laide, so we end our countdown.

Over my shoulder I'm aware that things are happening. The Warder, who should have been made of sterner stuff, has passed out. Or away. It's difficult to tell from where I am.

Some of the Americans, our own party among them, have run screaming. One old lady is fumbling frantically for her spectacles.

To my horrified ears comes the familiar tone of the croaking old man from Des Moines, Iowa: 'Well, I've heard of Son et Lumière, but this is ridiculous.'

Rupert Colt is not amused. It's almost as though we'd been caught spitting at the Crown Jewels, though, I suppose, in some ways that might not have been so bad. 'In the White Tower!!' he keeps repeating.

'For God's sake, Rupert. What difference does the colour make?'

She has a point.

That's not all she has, but let's not start all that up again. Otherwise I'll be off with the loofah myself.

I confidently expect to get the order of the boot, which will probably mean a speedy goodbye to Miss Loveband and my Cally Road paradise.

'You didn't do anything right. I blame you, Miss Laide. I fear you led this poor boy astray. You were supposed to be showing him the ropes. Taking him in hand.'

I cannot restrain a snigger.

He turns on me, his piggy little eyes flashing fire and slaughter. 'I can see you're not blameless, Jonny. I'm very disappointed in you. In fact, I fear I shall have to ask both of you to . . .'

Leonora holds up a hand, cutting him off in his prime. She strides over to him and almost lifts him off his dainty feet, carrying him into the inner sanctum. As she closes the door she gives me an encouraging wink.

I could do with forty such winks.

Inside, there is the raised voice of Rupert, starting very loud and going on up the scale. There is the sound of a slap, cracking out like a belch in a classroom.

There's more talk. Or, rather, it's mutter. I can't tell the difference. The temp and I sit looking at each other like a couple of spare ribs at a chef's wedding. The door opens and out comes Leonora Laide, smiling all over her voracious face.

'Don't worry, Jonny. It's all O.K. with Rupe the Loop. I've quit. No, I was going to anyway. Honest. I just reminded Mr Colt of a few facts of life. Like who does what to who and who tells who about it all. If you see what I mean.'

I don't. She might be giving me a lesson in algebra in Urdu for all the sense it makes. But I nod.

47

'You're very sweet, Jonny. Thanks for a really nice day today.'

And she kisses me gently on the lips and walks out of the tatty little office into the snow-covered streets. I never see her again.

Wherever you are, Leonora, thanks.

I bet there's not a dry eye among the readers now, is there? There is!! You hard-hearted swine!

I don't know what she tells Rupert, but it quietens him down a treat. When he calls me in, he's under control and he never mentions the Tower of London caper again.

'Never mind, dear boy. Never mind. Can happen to anyone, to be seduced by a woman . . . So I'm told. Incidentally, did I ever tell you the one about the gay spider?'

I can't believe that the storm has truly passed and that I'm still one of the great employed.

'No, Rupert, I don't believe you did tell me about the gay spider.'

Composure regained, his little chin (chins) begin to wobble with merriment. 'He was always after someone else's flies.'

CHAPTER FOUR

I am eating my ham and eggs at Bacon Hill. They are delicious. One thing I am lucky in – most of the birds that I have ever had the pleasure with have been fair hands in the kitchen.

Linda Loveband is no exception. There is only one big drawback – apart from the elephant's foreskin, which is an even bigger drawback – and that is her bleeding dog.

It is called 'Cheetah', for no reason that I have been able to discover and it is not fat. No, it is *gross*!! It lives for the days when we have an Italian supper, as it has an unhealthy taste for pasta. If I have my way, it will not live long enough to have any futura!

It is always insinuating itself between its mistress and my mistress (who are one and the same, in case you were getting confused) at moments of high passion.

But, that apart, Bacon Hill is turning out a vast improvement on Longlea Road. The house is big enough for me to stretch a bit and the others in the place seem quite nice. At the time of writing, the first floor is occupied by an amiable lunatic named Hugh James David Thomas. In his early middle-age, he is the black sheep of a landed Hampshire family, who is eking out a living by driving London Transport buses. By one of those amazing coincidences, which I don't expect you to believe, he has just applied for a job with Shuckburgh's, driving coaches.

Why do I call him an amiable lunatic? That's like asking 'What is Life?' There are so many reasons I could do you a nice little chapter just about the inimitable Thomas.

For instance, since you press me. One day he's bombing along through Holloway with a full load on board his double-decker, when a lorry cuts him up. Most men would be content with a blast on the horn and a fleeting Harvey through the windscreen.

Not Hugh James. He puts his foot down and thunders

off in hot pursuit. Ladies crying as they not only go past their stops, but way off the route. He finally sees the lorry parked down a side road and blocks it with the bus.

Sadly, an inspector makes him drive it back on the proper route. I ask him why they didn't try to stop him by ringing the bell.

'Oh, they did, Jonny,' with a broad grin through his tea-strainer moustache. 'I just pulled the wire out so I could get some peace and quiet.'

You like it? All right, here's another. I hear this from Linda, but you can still see the results, so I know she's telling the truth.

It's his turn to mow the tablecloth of grass, but the mower isn't working. Hugh James David Thomas takes the petrol tank off his moped and sprinkles it all over the lawn. Stands in the middle and throws down a match.

Whoooooooooooooooooooosssssssssssssssssssssssh!

Up goes the lawn and most of Hugh. 'Kept the grass down though, didn't it?' says he as they take off the bandages.

Linda once recommended that he try fish fingers, as he didn't eat very nutritiously. For the next five weeks he lived on NOTHING but fish fingers.

There was the time he decided to wash his tatty lace curtains. Boiled them for an hour in a bucket of bleach! The only way he could get them out was in spoonfuls of grey sludge. Lovely guy.

Amiable lunatic like I said. I've only been at Bacon Hill a month, but he's already left his double-decker bus parked outside, in a narrow little road, all night every night for a week. He couldn't be bothered to take it back to the garage and then have to walk all the way home every night!

That's the first floor. The second floor is empty but the top floor has a couple of single ladies sharing. I won't cast any aspersions, but if I was a little Dutch boy I'd watch where I was putting my finger while they're around!

Miss Loveband places a gentle hand on the muscle that cheers but doth not impregnate (hopefully!) and I nearly knock over my cup of coffee. The last few mouthfuls of fried bread mop up the delicious grease, and I lick my lips.

One minute later, I am again licking up a storm, when I feel a tap on top of the head. There must be a joke there, but I can't think of one. My ears are somewhat compressed by legs Loveband, which are rising and falling in time with the bedsprings.

'Jonny, love, I'm afraid there isn't time for that again this morning.'

Note the word 'again'. No point in false modesty, is there?

(Publisher's Note: Not where Jonathan May is concerned! 'Modesty' is not a word in his language.)

I have a quick wash and leap into my natty suiting, wondering whether to take the maroon or the black. Or the grey.

If you're awake, you'll be wondering how poor Jonny May has become the proud possessor of such a wardrobe.

Money. Like young Zimmerman says: It doesn't just talk, it swears.

The life of a travel courier is not an unrewarding one. That one day in London ending in the bloody Tower – and I do mean with a small 'b' – taught me a lot. How to pick up tips, not just from the punters, but from the owners of restaurants and clubs. Discounts everywhere.

Rupert has one little trick – not that, dear – he insists we use. At the end of each run round London we always finish up miles from the centre. I have to break the sad news that a fuel surcharge means that they have to pay again to travel back in the coach. Two pounds a head!

Most of them pay without a murmur. Those that murmur get a swift reading of the Rules and Regs (see earlier in the book), and the choice of walking or fighting for a taxi. Most would rather live on their wallets than die on their flat feet.

The month has gone well. Today is 17 March. Another Monday. I pass Hugh going out, all wrapped up in flying boots, sheepskin jacket, gauntlets, goggles, helmet and waterproof trousers. Ready to dice with death at sixteen miles an hour all the way to Holloway Bus Garage, a full mile if it's an inch.

One thing bugs me about Colt's Travel Agency. It still hasn't got me out of the country. In fact, it hasn't got me more than five miles from Charing Cross at any time. All round London tours. Every time I mention the Caribbean or the Costa Brava, the Costa Del Sol, or the Costa Blanco, he gets tight-lipped and moans about the Costa Living!

I shall never mingle with the millionaires. My brother Morrie is still out there, soaking up the sun. I know. I get his cards forwarded to me from my old address. All with postage owing.

I have no real idea where sister Melanie is. That's when I begin to worry. When I don't know. As long as she's in Hell, Hull or Halifax, I'm happy. The last card I got from her said she'd met a nice Corsican who was going to make her a star. If all the men who were going to make my sister a star were laid end to end, I wouldn't be a bit surprised.

Rupert is turning out to be a reasonable boss, if that isn't a contradiction in terms. Apart from when he gets a gleam in his eye and says: 'I feel like a new man.'

He's really been very tolerant, though he sometimes seems to be making a special effort for me. I wonder why. I also wonder how Morrie knows about me working in the travel business. Morrie works (or doesn't work) in a very mysterious way to perform some of his more dubious wonders.

No, I was talking about Rupert's tolerance. I have not yet been revealed as God's gift to the travel business. But I am confident that things must get better. By the Moor and the Cock! That qualifies for the Jenny Runacre Award for the Understatement of the Year.

Because I just happen to fancy Jenny Runacre, that's why. Then again, who wouldn't?

There was the sad affair of mistaken identity at Buckingham Palace. I mean, the Queen Mother is not very tall and not quite as slim as she once was. But, looking back on it, I'm forced to admit that it was a bit silly expecting to find her sweeping the corridor in a grey overall with a fag drooping from the corner of her mouth.

But there *was* a passing resemblance. Honest!

Then there was the business of that big stone in Westminster Abbey. I was taking this party of fellows in kilts round, and the next thing I knew they were trying to load this huge block of granite in the back of the coach. Claimed it reminded them of home.

I still think the judge was a bit harsh describing me as 'an easily-lead tool who'd been gulled into an act of criminal folly', and that only my youth had 'saved me from a more swingeing sentence'. I got bound over. It hurts less than being run over.

The evening paper described me as 'Jonas Mayerling', which relieved me. I didn't want me mum and dad to think I'd got into bad company.

My mum thinks that London is peopled only with junkies, hippies, Teddy Boys, greasers, strippers, ponces, gamblers, hookers, mods, perverts, rockers, gipsies, G.I.s, and cabinet ministers having affairs with ladies who are less good than they might be.

Then there was the confusion at Windsor. Well, how was I to know they were 'His' polo ponies. The Canadian lads seemed confident it'd be all right to ride them.

And maybe I shouldn't have given any advice to the Australians who wanted to know the best places for shop-lifting. But I really believed they were joking.

As for the greyhound, the vibrator, the Hungarian countess and the twin bathing beauties from Siam . . . the less said the better. Apart from mentioning that it got Colt's Tours banned from Kew Gardens in perpetuity.

Yes, folks, it's been an eventful month. Of course, there have been plenty of days that have gone like a dream. One of those dreams when you're trapped in a long corridor, with all the doors locked against you and a faceless creature coming slobbering after you!

Ones of those dreams.

On the leisure side, Elizabeth James has at last made it to London. Her husband – a writer who nurtured a secret ambition to be a Cost and Works Accountant, but couldn't make his flow charts flow – has settled enough on her to get her started in London, while he shacks up with a lady wrestler from Coventry.

Liz's got a pad for herself in Notting Hill. Furnished. If

that's the right word for the stuff the landlord leaves behind. It's lousy in every sense of the word.

But it's nice to see her. Although Linda is fine, I'm never one to think that a little variety is a bad idea. She's getting a job in publishing, being of an intellectual bent, so she should be in London for some time. I keep my fingers crossed that she keeps her legs open.

Maybe more of the lovely Liz later.

Back to 17 March and another day. What will it have to offer? I ask myself. Myself has learned better than to try and guess.

For once the tube runs all the way in without collapsing in a hissing of doors and a crackling over the loudspeakers with the glad news there's another along in a minute. Rupert is already there. As I walk in he is reading another of these bright postcards, which I imagine must be from his hordes of satisfied clients. Though, in a full month I have yet to see a single customer who got any satisfaction from Colt's. Unless you count the old man with the bad chest from Des Moines, Iowa, on my cataclysmic first day.

Looking as guilty as though he'd been caught stealing knickers from a magistrate's clothes line, he stuffs the card in his inside pocket before I have a chance to look at it properly. But I feel a nagging suspicion that the handwriting on the card was vaguely familiar.

'Aah, Jonny?'

Who's he expect? Ex-King Zog of Albania?

I smile and sit down at my desk. Today is one of the days that the temp is not going to turn up. I feel it in my bones. If you get one in for two days running, then you throw your cap over the moon and send out for the champers.

There's the usual pile of letters with complaints, including, I notice interestedly, one from Des Moines, Iowa. I dig out the form letters and sign them illegibly, speeding them off to all parts of the world.

No, I don't bother reading them. I mean, they get the same sort of sound and the same phrases in them. It gets boring.

You know, words like: 'Disgusted . . . Bitterly disappointed . . . Angry . . . Good thrashing . . . Advertisement for your country . . . Paternity suit will (What? Oh, that's for the Greek restaurant next door.) . . . Nervous breakdown . . . Never in my whole experieice . . .' And so on and on and on.

We have a range of replies. They start with: 'Many thanks for your interesting letter which will be investigated.' Another one says: 'Mr Colt is currently out of the country but will be in touch with you on his return.' Then we go on to: 'I'm afrade that I am the onlie on left hear and I don't now were any of them have gon and I can't stan it any longr.'

The last one, which is usually sent out in reply to the letters threatening legal action (eighty per cent), simply says: 'The business you mention has ceased trading for the time being. As soon as its financial affairs have been clarified, contact with all litigious parties will be made.'

While I finish that off, Rupert comes humming into the room, chewing a hot sausage French that he's actually gone out and got himself from Levy's. I say 'humming' because he's got on some new cologne he's treated himself to and it makes him smell different. Without it he pongs like a parrot's armpit. With it, he smells like a scented parrot's armpit!

He peers over my shoulder, dripping bits of hot sausage and crumbs of French all over my desk. With a limp flick of the wrist, he brushes them off, knocking half the letters on the floor at the same time.

'Whoopsie! Never mind. Let fallen complaints lie, I always say. Incidentally, did I tell you about the two gay lads who went for a day's outing to Battersea Fun Fair?'

I shake my head wearily and put down the pen. 'No, Rupert. You didn't. But, before you start, can we talk about me getting out of London and heading for somewhere a bit exotic and a bit different? I want new frontiers, Rupert. I want to try something I've never done before.'

For a moment a note of interest sparkles in his eyes, but he soon realises that I don't mean what he hopes I mean, and he carries on with his joke as though I haven't even spoken.

'Yes. Well, these two gay boys go to the fun fair and one

55

of them decides he wants to go on the roundabout. His friend stays where he is and tells him he'll wave as he goes by. Well, the first one – let's call him Jules – gets on and clutches his golden horse by the neck. His friend – let's call him Jimmy – stands at the side, ready to watch and wave. Right; off they go. But the moment it starts, the thing gets out of control. It whizzes round. Up and down. Round and round. Everything becomes a blur. People screaming.'

The telephone rings. Rupert ignores it.

'Finally, there's a vast explosion. Booooom! Horses and people and chunks of roundabout flying through the air. Jimmy goes running into the smoking debris and finally locates his friend Jules covered in beams and tangled metal. White-faced and trembling, Jimmy heaves him out and holds him in his arms. And says: "Are you hurt?"'

The telephone is still ringing for those of you who worry about that sort of thing.

' "Are you hurt?" asks Jimmy. Jules looks up at him. "Of course I am. You didn't wave." '

I have to admit that some of Rupert's collection of odd stories are sometimes not unamusing. Unfortunately, this is not one of those times.

I laugh dutifully and Rupert scuttles into his office and answers the phone.

'Yes . . . Who's that? . . . Who? Speak up. It sounds like you're shouting down a railway tunnel in Detroit . . . That's better . . . You what? Why? . . . How the hell am I?? I know that . . . All right, if you can't you can't . . . Right, I'll ring you back later . . . Byeee.'

A month at Colt's Tours has made me realise that when the telephone rings it is more often bad news than good. The look on Rupert's face when he comes back in convinces me that I'm right. He looks like Malcolm Allison on one of those days that Crystal Palace have gone down two-nil at home.

'Jonny, you said you wanted to get out of the office, didn't you?'

'Yes, yes I did.'

I can hardly contain myself. This must be it. The big

break-through. Millionaires' Row here I come. The cold wind that detours specially to go up one trouser leg and down the other stops worrying me. Only a matter of hours and I'll be on my way to the sun and the sea. I can almost feel the warm surf bubbling round my short and curlies.

'Can you speak Russian, Jonny?'

The warm sun vanishes behind a Siberian cloud.

'No, of course not. Why?'

Still, maybe it won't be that bad. Moscow, with the gold leaf on the Kremlin domes shining across Red Square. The bodies of the great Russian leaders embalmed like dead flies, caught forever in a crystal of amber. Forever amber, in fact. Lovely Russian spies offering me nameless vices in return for the secret of my mum's bread-and-butter pudding.

'You're taking over a tour by a party of Russian businessmen. Don't worry, though; I'm reliably informed that they'll have their own interpreter with them.'

Russian businessmen! Not another day round the sights of swinging London. The only thing worse than a wet Monday in March in London is a wet Monday in March in Birmingham.

'Where do I take them?'

'Birmingham!'

On the way north I buy a copy of a book to try and teach myself a few handy Russian phrases – like, 'You look tired, my little dove. Would you like to rest with me?'

Not so easy. I've forgotten that they have a different alphabet to us. I begin at the top of page one and find out that the 'The Russian alphabet is unusual in that it has thirty-two letters'.

That's enough for me.

I have an early lunch on the train. What they jokingly refer to as lunch. The water has the consistency of gravy. The soup has the consistency of water. The gravy has the consistency of mashed potato and the mashed potato has the consistency of custard.

But they sure make out a neat bill!

As I get off the train in Birmingham, the sun breaks through in a watery glow, welcoming me back to my old home town again. I haven't had time to warn my mum and dad of their prodigal's return. From the itinerary Rupert has laid on me I'll be lucky to find time to breathe.

It's not the sun. It's the street lights by the station that someone has left on by mistake. My welcome back comes the moment I step outside the station, when a pigeon decides to use me at his convenience. That should be 'as' his convenience.

When I get to the hotel I find the lobby full of red-faced Russians, all seemingly in the same tight-fitting suits. I quickly realise that they are not happy. Their guide didn't turn up, and they have already missed a tour of the ball-bearing factories of Smethwick and Wolverhampton. Doesn't the thought of that set the adrenalin pounding through your veins?

Nor me.

They're all gathered round, shouting and pushing at me. It's worse than being trapped by the hat counter in the Spring Sales at Stoppers. I can't understand a word any of them are saying, but it all seems to come through tightly-clenched teeth and involves screwing up the eyes in a sinister way.

I am beginning to wonder whether I'm going to be a tragic victim of the hotting up of the cold war, when I hear the cool tones of a woman cut through all the bedlam. Whoever she is, they all respect her, because there's instant silence.

In two shakes of a Pawnee's poker they've all slunk back into the dark shadows of the lobby, leaving me alone in the middle with . . .

'Galiana Ripemov.'

That's what it sounds like, but remember there are thirty-two letters in the Russian alphabet, and that may have suffered in the translation.

Galiana is the interpreter. What a bald statement of fact. She is a poem in passion. Shortish. Black hair, curling down to a broad pair of shoulders. A pair of sparkling eyes above a pair of sparkling knockers. Nice complexion. Close-fitting black woollen dress that keeps her warm and makes me very warm.

The prospect of a Russo-English entente makes Edgar cheer up, and he begins to behave like a rather vulgar boatman. Heaving and hoing all over the place. Galiana notices this and smiles at my obvious enthusiasm to get on the job. Damn it! On *with* the job.

I quickly make the apologies for the non-appearance of guide Number One.

'Plees do not vorry, Meester May. I am shure he vas not as nice as you.'

Actually, she doesn't really talk much like that. Her accent is excellent, with just the faintest hint around the 's' and 't' that she isn't British. So from now on I'll stop trying to put her accent in.

All I know is that the ball-bearing trip is definitely off. Rupert told me to play it by ear; so I do.

'I suppose you'll want to be getting off as soon as possible now,' I say, waiting for a clue as to where we're supposed to be going.

'Yes. My comrades are eager to commence.'

'Right. Good. Fine. Grand. Super.' I stand there like a spare tic at a neurologist's wedding, hoping something will come along.

It does. Galiana claps her hands and jabbers away to her compatriots. They all stop arguing among themselves and file dutifully forwards. I notice all the men have big wide-brimmed hats. Like stetsons after a horse has trodden on them. And the ladies all wear head-scarves and big boots. They look like the pictures I used to see of Russian lady street-sweepers.

'Incidentally, Miss Ripemov, what exactly is this party?'

'Members of the Moscow and district highway cleansing departments.'

What that means is that they're street cleaners.

'I suppose we will not need a coach. I have made enquiries

at the desk, and I am told it is only a short walk.'

'Yes. Oh, yes. That's right.'

Where is only a short walk? By Japetus and Andromeda! I can see nasty times ahead for Jonny if he doesn't get his digit extracted in rapid time.

With a muttered excuse about a little dog, which leaves her blank-faced, I stroll up to the reception desk. There lounges the pride and joy of Balsall Heath, picking his teeth with a chipped match-stick.

People coming to the Midlands for the first time are surprised by the accent. That is, they can't understand a word the locals say. This is because it does have a certain thickness, being mainly expressed at the back of the throat, with the words struggling for survival all the way up the nose and out through the mouth. Any attempt to reproduce it in this book would be doomed to failure, so I won't try.

If you know what it sounds like, it won't matter. If you don't, then imagine someone sounding like he's going to gob on your Axminster. Then you'll get the general idea.

'Yes. What do you want?' This is with the match-stick still deep in a cavity the size of the Bull Ring. (Birmingham landmark ruined by planners.)

'Where are the Russian party supposed to be going this afternoon?' I ask politely.

'I don't give a monkey's.'

I rap my fingers gently on the top of the desk. My patience runneth over. I lean across the desk and grasp the pimpled youth by the collar, twisting it so that his face becomes an interesting shade of puce.

'Listen, smiley. Unless you want your knees nailed to the floor, you'd better tell me where they're going.'

I let him go, and his face becomes an interesting shade of yellow. 'You didn't have to do that,' he whines.

'Quite true, squire,' I beam. 'I could simply have pushed your teeth through the back of your neck.'

'All right, all right. They're supposed to be going to the Art Gallery.'

In fact his message is concealed behind a lot of words

that begin either with 'f' or 'c', but I've left them out to avoid boredom.

'Thank you, sonny,' I say, flipping his tie loose from its perch.

You will note that a month working in Soho has taught me more about the seamy side of life than a year at Stoppers did.

I rejoin the party, face wreathed in smiles.

'Come then,' I say gallantly to Galiana, offering her my arm. And orf we jolly well go.

They love it, though I suspect one or two of them think it's all a bit decadent and bourgeois. Then again, some of them are so prejudiced they'd probably think a public lavatory was decadent and bourgeois. I hand out leaflets and send them scurrying off to all corners of the Museum and Art Gallery.

When I used to live in Brum I was often disappointed to find that there were ten times the number of tourists in the Gallery than there were local folk. Shame, because there's some nice things in there.

Galiana obviously feels that she should be with her charges, but I maintain a vice-like grip on her arm and steer her to quieter pastures. The only man who follows us is a decrepit old dotard in a huge black cloak.

Try as I might I can't shake him off our tail. Maybe he's an agent from OGPU or SMERSH. I suss out fast that he's not a ballet dancer who wants to defect.

We stroll past a lot of stuffed birds. Sorry, here comes a short side-track. I remember being in the Beacon Cinema, Great Barr watching 'Psycho'. Remember it? Nutty Tony Perkins is talking about his hobby. He rolls his eyes coyly and says: 'I stuff birds.' That got the second biggest laugh I ever heard at the Beacon. The biggest was when a cigarette-end was flicked from the balcony and lodged down the back of the ice-cream lady's uniform.

We used to call her 'Twin-tub Tessie'. After the quickest striptease (very little of the tease about it), we renamed her 'Freda Flasher'. There was another name as well, but it's too rude to repeat.

Galiana and I are getting quite friendly, if it wasn't for this doddering old goat who keeps asking questions, after looking them up in a phrase book he must have looted from the Czar's Palace.

It has phrases in it like: 'My cuspidor has overflowed.' And: 'My kedgeree has been inadequately warmed.'

It's nice and warm, and I offer to carry Galiana's coat for her. Suddenly, out of the darkness behind us, I hear: 'Cloak! Cloak!'

Hello! I think. A Chinese frog's escaped.

No. It's Doctor Lumbago wanting me to carry his cloak for him. We are at the top of a flight of stairs at the time, and I contrive to drop it all the way down to 'Fossils'. He goes hopping after it, cursing fluently in Serbo-Croat.

Galiana and I melt into the shadows. We pause in front of a nice Pre-Raphaelite picture of some under-dressed ladies lounging around a table. I know it's Pre-Raphaelite because a chinless twit with a crowd of kids in tow is squawking on about it at the top of his tedious voice. I am delighted to see some bright child has stuck a little notice on Sir's back. It says: 'Danger! Bore at Work!'

The Museum is nice and quiet, and we whisper sweet nothings to each other. Without any warning she takes me by the back of the head and pulls my face down to hers. I kiss her softly, and she tastes fresh and clean. Just a hint of mint.

Edgar is ready to sniff the open air again, and I move a bit so that Galiana can feel it. She giggles. 'Is that a pen-knife in your pocket, or are you just glad to see me?'

Where we are strolling is pitch dark. I think that there must be a power failure and am using the blackness to have a quick squeeze at the titskis, or whatever they're called in Russia.

If anyone had rammed a hot poker up my bum, I doubt if I'd have jumped more. Galiana screams, and goes limp. No, not like a cripple. Limp and faint.

There's a crack of thunder, and the whole room where we are is lit with a ghastly green brilliance. Ten feet away from us, jaws open and roaring like my old man when he put oven-cleaner on his pork chop by mistake, there's this sodding huge DINOSAUR!!!!!!

Honest.

If you've ever been to Birmingham Museum, then you'll know I am, as always, telling the truth, the whole truth and some things as well as the truth.

Tyrannosaurus Rex. That's what the notice says, when I've stopped my heart palpitating enough to be able to read it. It's a life-size model, complete with cracking roar and flashing eyes.

I'm surprised they don't put up a big notice offering a thousand pounds to anyone who dies of fright in the place. Trouble is, they'd probably have every fly boy in the city bringing their weak old mums and dads along on the off-chance.

I bring Galiana round with my special May version of the kiss of life. She perks up, and takes an even greater interest in the exhibits. The one she likes best is an example of methods of erection of dwellings. Her greatest interest is reserved for one method of erection in particular. If I tell you that the method is called 'Edgar' I doubt that any of you will be at all surprised.

There's a lecture theatre, with a sign saying: 'The Future of Tomorrow'. Sounds interesting, and we shuffle in, narrowly dodging the old peasant peering at a stuffed gorilla and baring his teeth at it. When you see his fangs, you stop wondering where the yellow went.

Inside the lecture room there's the warm, familiar smell of dusty velvet. There's only one dim bulb glowing up in the roof, and I notice a notice. By the door, just inside. It says: ' "Tomorrow" has been cancelled owing to lack of interest.'

I'm about to walk out again, when I feel chubby fingers tampering with my sex sausage. In one shake of a cossack's hassock we are intertwined on the steps of the theatre, with her ripping my clothes from my unprotesting person and whistling quietly under her breath.

63

I've heard of Russian steppes, but this is ridiculous. And uncomfortable. With the edge sticking into my back. We shuffle about like two halves of a pack of cards, until we get a reasonable position.

After everything I've read about the cold Russians, I am shocked to find Galiana Ripemov going on like this. I reciprocate her attentions. I feel a right tit, and then a left one. My other hand is ferreting around under layer after layer of petticoats. It's like trying to unpack a new shirt in the dark.

A wriggle and a change in pitch of the whistle tells me I'm homing in on target. My moving finger moves, and having moved moves on. And up. And, finally, in. Naughty decadent silk pants give way to a curly curtain. Part that and find the start button.

I come into harbour as smoothly as Chay Blyth ever did. It's not the best place to do thingie in that I've ever come across (if you'll pardon the expression) and I must say that I would prefer to have had a bed under my Red. Still, we manage all right and the lecture theatre resounds to groans and little Russian cries of exultation.

For once it all goes well. No tourists. No noises to put us off. Edgar puts up a performance that should help Anglo-Russian relations for generations, if there's any justice. Which there isn't, of course.

That's all there is to say. We rejoin the rest of the party. The Communist party. We make a few formal speeches to each other and everyone claps everyone else. Galiana gives me a rouble for a keepsake and tells me to look her up any time I'm in Moscow.

On the train back to London I think over the day and reckon it's been one of my better ones. I came out on top. Well, I suppose alternative positions are frowned on in Russia.

And I know a Russian phrase. Galiana shouted it out just as we were . . . you know, don't you? It means . . . well, what you'd expect it to mean at such a time.

Roughly translated, it means 'Ram your ***** harder into me. Let me feel your ***********'.

Only thing is, I can't think of any occasion that *I* could ever use it.

Also, I can say 'Goodbye'. Do widzenia.

(Publisher's Note: Actually, that's Polish, but we didn't like to tell him.)

CHAPTER FIVE

Author's Note: I knew it was Polish, so there. I do all my writing with a John Bull printing outfit and it doesn't run to Russian letters!

Rupert is pleased with my efforts in London, and I get what he considers rewards. Like four days in Hull with eighty-seven Danish fishing experts. Like a day trip to Scunthorpe with three Americans who were born there. This is one of Rupert's less successful ideas.

I take forty jolly French housewives on a draggy coach ride to Huyton. When we get there, they start asking where the Royal Pavilion is. Hugh James David Thomas has now joined us as driver and it is his quick wit that spots we should have gone to Brighton. If he'd listened properly to his instructions, we might have done.

But still no sun and sand and cool drinks and gleaming, dusky bodies. If I wait long enough I can get it all in Britain. The summer, as it is sometimes called, will not be that long in coming.

It is now 3 April. Birthday of Marlon Brando and Doris Day. Now there's a coincidence. If you watch telly commercials you'll know that Miss Day uses a lot of margarine. Whereas Mr Brando only used butter!

I'm sure you'll want to know how things are going on what we might call the Edgar front. I mean, he's hardly at the back, is he?

Elizabeth James is busy with her job and is getting ready for her holiday. I try to persuade her to take a Colt Special, but she thinks better of it. Or, do I mean worse of it? Either way, she ain't going.

Linda Loveband is proving everything a landlady's daughter should be, with that bit extra that counts. Trouble is, she's met a fellow at work, and is actually thinking of getting married. Ugh! The mention of the word makes me feel faint. I tell her it will mean the end of our beautiful relationship, but she reckons her husband-to-be won't mind.

Greater love hath no man than that he lays down his wife for another.

In fact Edgar has been short of nooky at Bacon Hill for a week or so owing to an unfortunate error on my part. I am running the bath – the bathroom is at the end of the hall – when the phone rings. I carefully avoid the bare wire where Hugh James David Thomas has been doing one of his famous repairing jobs.

I come in that evening and he stops me in the hall. 'Look here, Jonny,' he says. 'Watch out for that live wire by the phone. I've been fixing it. If you touch it, like this aieeeeeee eeeeeeeeee!!!!!!!!' he rises four feet in the air and comes crashing down with his right arm shaking like he's just had a nasty shock. When he stops shaking, he says: 'Hey, I just had my hand on a thousand vôlts.' 'How much is that in English money?' I say heartlessly.

The phone is ringing. I wrap a towel round me and answer it. It is the lovely Elizabeth James telling me she's having trouble booking her holiday, but intends to get to Rome, if she can.

We chatter on about this and the other. She has a sexy voice and Edgar struggles against the restraint of the towel. I suppose the call's been going on for about a quarter of an hour.

The front door opens and in comes Linda. She's been shopping and is looking very good in a new coat, new shoes and a new dress. Even Cheetah has had a shampoo and looks marginally less repulsive than usual. I wave a hand and terminate the conversation. Bad form to gossip to a lady friend in front of another. Anyway, I reckon Edgar is due to be taken for a walk under the pussy pelmet.

Alas for human pride and ambition! Linda wants a leak and goes into the bathroom.

She opens the door.

'Something's holding it shut,' she says.

That's the moment that I remember that I have forgotten . . . forgotten to turn the taps off in the bathroom.

Linda finds out before I can tell her. She finds out by heaving the door open.

A tidal wave sweeps down the hall, breaking against the front door. It knocks Linda clean off her feet and deposits her on her cute little bottom in two feet of steaming water. The abominable Cheetah is carried yelping the whole length of the corridor, a frightened and soggy hot dog.

Where I'm standing I miss most of the wave, and I'm dressed for it anyway. Looking back on it I can see now that it was an error of judgement on my part to start laughing. A cringing apology would have been more in order.

'Hope those clothes are drip-dry,' I quip.

There's many a quip . . . She gets up, wipes the water and steam from her glasses and begins to walk in a slow menacing way down the hallway.

I wave my hands at her in a manner that I hope will placate her. 'Listen, love. It was an accident. I'll clean it up. It'll dry out all right. Sooner or later. Or, do I mean sauna or later?'

Miss Loveband is not amused. First she throws one wet shoe at me, making sure I feel the heel. Then the other, which is not good for the sole. I'm feeling on my uppers now and begin to worry for the safety of my cobblers. I leap nimbly into the bathroom and slam the door on her advancing figure.

I shout through the keyhole: 'Don't worry, Linda. I'll make it all up to you in bed.'

Her voice has a cold venom that I have not heard since I last saw Jack Palance gun down Elisha Cook Junior in 'Shane'.

'If you come anywhere near me tonight . . . or any other night, Jonathan May, I will not answer for the consequences.'

Since most of the water in the bath is cooling I decide to drain it and start all over again. The noise of the water drowns most of her words, while she goes on at sickening length about her plans. I still hear enough to make Edgar shrink back into his shell.

'Stretch it with . . . Jump with my high heels . . . with the razor . . . Nail it to . . . Sliced on toast . . . bury it at a crossroad at midnight with . . .'

So it was several nights' solitary for Jonny. I think that I've got back into her good books by getting Cheetah some tins of his favourite dog-food. I leave it outside her door with a jolly note. 'Next time I have a bath, I'll give you plenty of warning so that you can get in your eighty cubits of gopher wood.'

It can't fail.

It can fail.

I forget that it's raining outside and her glasses tend to get misted up. I hear her walk in. Close the front door. Stumble with an unladylike curse. Clatter. Clatter. Scream from dog as heavy foot descends uncontrollably on tail. Scream as said dog bites mistress. Mine as well as his. More cursing. More clattering as lady falls over tins. Barking of ankles and of dog.

Time for me to rush out and help the fallen damsel. I open my door and step out into the hall. Linda Loveband is flat on her back nursing a bite on her shapely calf and showing a stupendous amount of laddered tights, surrounded by scattered tins of 'Dogilove'.

With controlled hatred, she spits out: 'Jonny, dear. Did you leave this death trap here, right where I could fall over it?'

This is the moment. I will make an abject apology. Tell her how sorry I am. Offer her anything to make it up to her.

That is what I intend. The kind, honeyed phrases are already forming themselves in the back of my mind, waiting to march smartly forward and step off my tongue to placate her.

Alas for good intentions! The road to chastity is paved with them. These kind words are too slow. My streak of malign fun gets there first.

My mouth droops open in a huge vacant grin.

69

'Enjoy the trip?' I say.

Back again to 3 April. You remember! Doris Day and Marlon Brando. Right. I walk into the tourist office supreme ready for what the day might offer. If it's another Mothers' Meeting from Coventry who want a male stripper and pick on me as the next best thing, I'll quit. I couldn't bare it again.

Without looking up, Rupert tosses me a brochure. 'Your next assignment,' he grunts.

I pick it up, expecting to find Colt's Conducted Tour of Norfolk mountains. That's the sort of unlikely thing that Rupert runs.

Has it occurred to you to wonder how this establishment keeps going? I've wondered too. You see, hardly any of the packages can be bringing in much money. And there are these odd cards that send Rupert whirling into a tiny tizzy. With the handwriting that always seems so familiar, but I never get the chance to see it properly. I found out, purely by snooping – I mean, by accident – that there is a large warehouse registered to the firm down in Wapping. Adjacent to the garage where most of the coaches are serviced.

I reckon that it's about time I raised it.

Dear, dear, dear . . . you can't say anything to some folks, can you? Edgar would be flattered to know that you were thinking of him, but I wasn't. I meant, raise the subject of the mysterious travel agency for which I work.

But this brochure distracts me. In full frontal colour, it is for a firm called Nudi-Tours, and that's what it is. This must be the only travel handout that you could buy under the counter at a Soho porn-shop. Printed in Denmark, it advertises various 'unusual' holidays in the sun.

'*This* is my new job?' I squeak unbelievingly.

Still without looking up, Rupert nods. 'Yes. You said you wanted to get abroad. Make the most of it though. This one might turn out to be a flash in a pan.'

This is a very unfortunate thing for him to say as I am just looking at a picture of some well-endowed fellow busy barbecuing a steak over a charcoal grill. Naturism is all very well, but I think I'd want to wear an apron for that job. I personally don't fancy having my flash end up in the pan. I'd end up with a jumping Edgar flash, and it would be far from a gas, gas, gas.

'Great, Rupert. Don't worry, I'll try to keep my end up for the old firm.'

Alas for proud ambition!

At last he looks up. There is a nasty bruise at the top of his nose, and the sunglasses he has taken to wearing lately have one lens starred.

'What's the matter?' I ask, at the same moment as he snaps 'Don't ask what happened.'

I say 'Sorry, I won't' at the same time that he says 'Well, all right. If you must know, I had an accident while I was kissing my friend good night.'

My brain selects the following words and begins to transmit them to my mouth: 'What happened then? Did she/he cross his/her legs and break your glasses?'

The May censor is just in time. (Relative of just in de villeneuve.) I strangle the thought and make noises indicating I'm sorry and what a pity and I hope he gets well soon.

He glances at my desk and his face goes all red and saggy, like a balloon on the way down. 'Who gave you that?' he rages, pointing at the brochure of lovely people doing lovely things.

'You gave it to me. It's my next job.' My protest checks his wrath.

'Oh. My mistake, Jonny. Ha, ha, ha.' His laughter is as hollow as a priest's hole. I always thought that was a bit of a contradiction. I mean, shouldn't it really be a nun's hole?

'Well, if it's not for me, who is it for?'

Blush, blush he goes. 'Actually, I'm thinking of having a bit of a break later in the year and I . . . er . . . um . . . you know?'

Yes I do. There's loyalty for you. A travel agent going off on someone else's tour. And a dirty tour at that. It's like Mary Whitehouse getting a season ticket to the Raymond Revuebar for a present from her family.

Reluctantly I give him back the leaflet, waving a fond farewell to all those acres of bouncing flesh. Still, maybe it's all for the best. I'm not sure that naturism is in my bag. I reckon that Edgar would prefer to remain in *his* bag.

I am now really unhappy with life and Rupert Colt. There are lots more jobs in this world, and I fancy having a go at some of them in the near future.

Rupert spots that I am not pleased. Perhaps it's the way I'm moodily carving a little gallows in the top of my desk.

'You ... you could always come with me, Jonny. Maybe you'd like it.'

'I'll be buggered if I go on holiday with you, Rupert.'

Like the prophets say, there is many a true word spoken in jest. Fortunately Rupert fails to notice my little faux pas.

By the way ...

(Publisher's Note: Oh, no. Here we go again.)

By the way, it seems this butler once asked his master the definition of the phrase faux pas. His master thought a bit and said: 'Well, Rabb, you remember when we had the Bishop of Grantchester to tea with Lady Windermere?' Rabb, the butler, nods. 'You remember how the Bishop caught his finger on a rosebush when they were walking in the garden before you served tea?'

'Yes, sir. I do.'

'Well, after that, while you were actually carrying round the tea tray, you remember that Lady Windermere leaned across and said to the Bishop peering at his injured finger: "I hope that is not infected. I have never seen a prick so red and swollen." You remember that?' The butler nods again. 'Well, Rabb, when you dropped the tea tray, *that* was a faux pas!'

During that brief intermission our sales staff visited all parts of the auditorium.

'But, Rupert,' I say. 'If that's not my next assignment, then what is?'

'This.'

'This' is a sheet of paper, badly typed. It's a list of names, headed 'Italy, Switzerland, Holland and France in ten days, stopping at Rome, Zurich, Amsterdam and Paris. The holiday of a lifetime'.

I see it is in co-operation with Sphere Travel; a reliable little outfit just up Gray's Inn Road. It crosses my mind that Rupert might be taking this on just to maintain his front.

I'm about to ask him, when it occurs to me that I am actually going abroad! !

'All right then, Jonny. Knew you'd like it. Start first thing tomorrow. I'll go over all your little details this afternoon. I'm just off for a hot sausage French.'

A draught from the door, and he's gone. For once he hasn't even given me a gay joke to exit on.

I sit there thinking about the great times to come in the next eleven days. I notice that the driver is H. J. D. Thomas, which takes a little of the icing off my cake.

Who can this assorted band of courageous travellers be who are going to place their happiness in my hands over the next few days?

The list gives names and addresses. They are entitled to a group discount, as they are all members of an organisation called 'Beer-quaffers Anonymous'. I don't like the sound of it.

I run my fingers down the list. None of them seem to be married. At least none of them are listed as taking wives with them. There is only one lady on the list, and she's right at the bottom. Very uncomfortable.

Let's see . . . they sound more like a conclave of gangsters than respectable businessmen . . .

Robert White . . . I'd have thought he'd have gone to the Costa Blanco. Frank Childs . . . must be Mary's boy! Don Goodall and Eddie Lamb . . . bet he's got a tale to tell.

Actually it's rotten of me to make jokes about other people's names. But at least I don't mind if anyone makes jokes about my name.

He lied.

Who else is there? Ron Spooner, Derek Ainge, Malcolm Thomas and Roy Wood. I wonder if he's a wizard with women! Don Read, Frank Price, Malcolm Turner, Graham

Hyett, Jim Campbell (obviously Welsh that one) and Mike Calver.

Here's another Welshman – Stuart Dalgleish. And yet another one – Jim McGarry. Wait a minute; that name is very familiar. No, it's gone. I'm sure I've heard of him in other spheres.

David Kent, Ken O'Neill. And John Abel. Must watch him; he'll always be raising Cain!

That's the lot.

My guess is that they're all nice blokes. Typical. Almost representative.

And, one woman. Mrs Elizabeth James.

Mrs Elizabeth James!

Mrs Elizabeth James!!!!!!

Lucky Jonny. I suppose she booked in and didn't realise the ghastly truth – that she's on a Colt Tour after all. I see she's only going as far as Rome. Never mind, it'll get the trip off on the right foot. I wouldn't say she was the sexiest lady with whom I've ever had the pleasure. Wait a minute! Yes I would. She makes Bardot look like Lord Longford in drag.

So tomorrow I'll be off. Apart from the nineteen blokes and Liz, I see that the numbers will be made up with overspill from other tours to bring the total to sixty-nine.

By the Cave and the Priest! That's a lot. Sixty-nine. Might be interesting when we get to France though. I do like a bit of the soixantes. Practise being a cunning linguist. Trouble is I tend to get in over my head.

Oh, all those lovely jests were to no avail. It's a typing mistake. It's actually *thirty*-nine. Never mind; I'll leave the jokes in anyway.

Waste not, want not. That is the motto of an aunt of mine. I'm not saying she's mean, but she is the only person I know whose notepaper is perforated and has 'Medicated With Izal Germicide' all across it.

Tonight Caledonian Road. Tomorrow Europe. I hope the markets aren't *too* common!

CHAPTER SIX

The coach trip down to Rome is truly horrendous! Half the people are late. Some are drunk – I will not name names here to cover up for the guilty. Two have forgotten their passports. One is on the wrong coach from the wrong firm on the wrong day going to the wrong countries.

The Channel is as calm as any narrow stretch of water when there is a Force Eight gale blowing. I realise that I am not one of the best sailors in the world. One of the jolly party from Sphere Travel keeps falling over me as I lie on the floor of the gents' toilet on the ferry, begging to die. Each time he says : 'Don't worry. Nelson was always sick.'

You know the sort of person I mean. The one who stuffs down a plate of cold fried eggs and a greasy chop just when you think you might be getting better.

It has been my hope to spend a bit of time cuddling up in the courier's compartment with Mrs James. I should be so lucky! I actually wanted to go on this sort of trip. I can't get over my own innocence and stupidity. It's like 'Emergency Ward Ten', 'Camp on Blood Island' and 'The Goodies' all rolled into one.

For a start: What a start! When Rupert tells me it would be an early start, I think he means about eight in the morning. Not so. He means *two* o'clock in the morning at Trafalgar Square.

My last night for a fortnight at Bacon Hill is wrecked. My trusty crossbow hardly has time to shoot its bolt before it's up, up and away. I snatch a goodbye kiss from the slumbering Linda, and leap into my waiting taxi, loaded with all sorts of travel pills, phrase books and more of Rupert's damned itineraries.

Then, once we're off the ferry, things don't get any better. I find myself in the centre of a threesome. On my right, Mr White is tucking into a jam roll. On my left, Mr Childs is eating a custard tart. Up front, Hugh James David Thomas is chatting up a girl from Surbiton who is coming on the trip to broaden her horizons. If she stays anywhere near Thomas, that isn't all that'll get broader.

There's a screech of brakes and the coach lurches to the right. In his eagerness to lay the ground to lay the lady dear Thomas has momentarily forgotten that he's no longer in England's green and pleasant land.

You're right; he was on the left.

The lurch deposits the Addams family of Twickenham on the floor. (That sentence contains a joke for followers of children's television. I thought I'd let you know so that you can drive yourselves nutty trying to work it out.)

Mr White's jam roll crunches into my right ear, while my left ear is filled with Mr Childs' custard tart.

I feel a trifle deaf.

One puncture and hundreds of miles further on we are at last nearing the eternal city. Not Manchester; Rome. It's hissing down with rain and the view from the window is as appetising as a cold cup of coffee filled with fag ends.

Bleak fields and a dirty dawn.

I know my duty as a good courier. Keep the customers happy at all times. Don't let their spirits flag. Mine are already at half-mast, but I rally. Honest; I really rally. Truly.

'Come on! Let's have a sing-song!' I bellow into my microphone.

A chorus of groans and curses greets my cheerful sally. Why don't I keep quiet and join Elizabeth in the back of the coach? Because I am a loyal and determined employee of Rupert Colt.

Actually it's because she has a rotten headache and is trying to sleep it off so that we can have a little fun before we part in Rome.

The lads from Sphere are more than happy to join in a sing-song. Unfortunately they insist on choosing the ditties, and some of them are not pretty ditties. They could put them on an L.P. called 'Songs That Even Rugby Players Would Blush At'.

When they get to the eighth verse of a hideous ballad

about a crab that is kept overnight in a maiden's chamber-pot, I finally have to draw the line.

'Gentlemen! Gentlemen!!' I yell. 'There are ladies aboard this coach!'

'Great! Let's be having them!' shouts a nameless individual from the safe darkness. In passing I wish that Shuck-burgh's had equipped their coaches wth those seats where you press a button and they eject the occupant up in the air like a Russian moon-shot.

Time passes on leaden wellingtons.

The coach rumbles on its way, broken only at intervals when a pale-faced lady has to get out and be sick, and for the frequently repeated cries of 'Does the driver want a wee-wee?' coming from a party that I won't mention.

An Irish gentleman with a glittering eye is narrating a lengthy tale of leprechauns and banshees. I listen with half an ear, until it starts to frighten me too much.

Elizabeth comes and sits by me which makes things look brighter. Even Edgar wakes up a bit. It is somewhat chilly, so I put my hands where I can warm them up and she does the same. Half an hour or so passes in this mutual pastime. Sadly it is pastime for me to be in bed, and I begin to nod.

'Why on earth do we have to do this trip in this way, Jonny? We're going all the way to Rome and then we've got to move on. They're fantastic distances. It's all right for me. I don't go any further than Rome, but it's going to be hell for the rest of you.'

Now she mentions it, I suppose it is an odd itinerary. Most tours of cities would either do Northern Europe *or* Southern Europe. We'll have run up a massive mileage by the time we get home again.

The discussion in the coach has turned to the more doubt-ful pleasures of Rome. This is one thing that Colt Tours are good at, and I have been well-briefed on the subject. I begin to lecture the lads on what and what not to do.

I warn them of the ladies of the Appia Antica. Some of them are so decrepit you reckon that they've been picking up travellers ever since they drove by in chariots. There are also some right old scrubbers near the Baths of Caracalla.

77

Still, at prices in the region of seventy-five pence, what do you expect?

Don't answer that.

One of the high-spots of low-life is the massage ladies. They double as manicurists, but if you asked them to trim your nails they'd look at you as though you were a right pervert.

I don't understand what they want so much information about tarts for. It's like going to Brighton, and spending all your time in a smoky Bingo Hall. If you want a paid lay, you can get it in London. And it's safe to drink the water in London.

Some of the coach party are absolutely loaded down with guide books and cards for each city we're going to spend a day in. Colt's advise a set tour in each place, but I wouldn't stick to it. It could be said that it's a bit old-fashioned. For instance, the Berlin tour advises sightseers to make sure they have plenty of coffee and cigarettes to barter with and to avoid the worst of the bomb-damage.

I haven't seen the one for Copenhagen, but it probably gives times to go and listen to Hans Christian Andersen (or Danny Kaye, as he's better known) making up fairy stories.

It may surprise you – I'm sure it will surprise a lot of you – but Jonathan May is a seeker after culture. I can't wait to visit the great galleries of all the places we're going to. Soak up the atmosphere of foreign parts. There's nothing like soaking up a foreign part, missus. Seriously though, I'm not going to have nothing to show for my time but a load of dirty pictures and the suspicion that that rash might be . . .

I came, I sore, I just cured.

I hear two of the young bloods discussing the possibility of ladies of the night putting out for free. If you believe that pigs can fly, then you might believe in the whore with the heart of gold. They're not called brasses for nothing, you know.

'Listen. I had a mate who saw this tart who could do this trick where she picked up a . . .' (A lorry thunders by in the night and I miss the rest of the lady's skill.)

'What? Even a fifty pence bit?'

'*Only* fifty pence bits.'
'Where does she hang out?'
'Somewhere up north.'
'Genoa?'
'No. I told you, I never even met her.'

The hotel isn't quite as shown in the prospectus.. At a quick glance, through sunglasses, in a thick fog, you might be lucky enough to catch a passing resemblance. Still, the only consolation is that we aren't going to be there long enough to worry much.

Most of the coachload have had a kip during the long long route across Europe. Apart from me and Hugh. Don't write in and tell me he shouldn't have done that all in one go and that it's against the law. I know.

He's been lucky enough to pull the young chick he was talking to, and intends to spend all of his Roman holiday in bed.

I crash out in my room. I could say that it's not very big. You have to stand on the bed to open the door! It seems as though one and a half seconds have passed when there's a thunderous knocking at the door, and some third-rate Valentino impersonator is telling me it's breakfast time. I need to know that like I need a hole in the head. Come to think of it, my head does feel as though someone's been using it for roller-skating practice during the splinters of night that were left.

I order eggs, bacon, fried bread, baked beans, porridge, toast, marmalade and a pot of white coffee. The waiter smiles vaguely and exits.

Sleep wraps me up in her warm overcoat again. Next time arrows of light dig into my eyeballs, he's back. I sit up ready to do justice to a manly meal. None of your continental breakfast crap. Rolls and black coffee. It might be all right for monks.

Luigi backs out, spotting that Jonathan May is not the great tipper of all time. My idea of a good tip is 'Simon Rack' in the third at Kempton Park. I lie back, close my eyes and inhale hard, ready to catch the odour of my nosh-up.

Odour! What can the matter be?

It's monk food. I had a mate who ran a fish-and-chip shop inside a monastery. He was the Chief Friar! Actually he was an ordinary chipmonk.

No. My breakfast is a stale roll and a pat of butter that wouldn't get you far if you were last tangoing in Cleethorpes, never mind Paris. And black coffee.

I have a packet of mints in my pockets. The ones with the less fattening centres. Better than nothing. On the strength of that I sally forth.

Did you know that God said to Moses: 'Come forth and win my eternal love', but he came fifth and won an electric toaster.

In the lobby about half of the party are sitting around looking like a load of spare wicks at a candle-maker's wedding.

Friend of mine used to work in a candle-making factory. Packed it in. Got fed up with the same old thing, wick in wick out!

Elizabeth has not appeared.

We are due to leave during the night, and sleep in the coach as it makes its perilous way to Switzerland. This means that I am not going to have any time to spend with her if I'm shepherding a crowd of clowns all over the city of seven hills. A fat lot of good going and throwing hard cash into a bleeding fountain. It's not Rome I want to come back to; it's Mrs James and her varied charms.

Fear not, Jonny is up to it.

'Right, gather round. Those who aren't here will have to make their own way, because I'm not going to hang about waiting. This will be our tour for the morning.'

There is a rumble of discontent. I glare round, until another rumble clues me in that it's my guts moaning about the rotten passage they're getting. But I also see that many of my cheerful clients aren't ... cheerful.

'What's wrong?'

It is one of the men who answers. 'Well. It's bloody peeing

down out there. We've seen the itrinarerariey thing, and we don't reckon it much.'

I mutter a swift prayer to my guardian angel. This is what I was hoping for.

I feign anger. Difficult when I'm rooting for them and not me. 'What do you mean? We're offering you a fine walk. Piazza Venezia to the Church of Santa Maria d'Aracoeli near the Capitol. Back down again through the via San Pietro to the via dei Fori Imperiali.'

Note how the words roll off my tongue. Liz and I weren't just holding . . . hands at the back of the bus. She speaks most European languages like a fish. That's not right, is it? Like someone who speaks most European languages well.

I see a look of blank despair creeping over the faces of my audience. I pitch my voice lower, like a hypnotist I once saw at the Aston Hippodrome. Low and monotonous.

He was very good this bloke. 'Professor Mesmer, the Master of the Orient', he was called. My old man said it was a load of cobblers and went up on the stage to prove it. The professor told him that he was a proud stallion.

My old man whinnied, threw his head back and went leaping out of the theatre. The police found him two hours later on the plinth of the statue of the Duke of Wellington on horseback. If I told you what my old man was trying to do to that bronze horse you would find it hard to believe. My old man just found it hard.

I drone on: 'We walk to the via dei Fori Romani and climb the steep hill to the Colosseum and then walk to the Piazza di Spagna, past the Trevi Fountain . . .'

The skinny girl from Purley begins to hum 'Three Coins in the Fountain' and a buzz begins of how they're at least looking forward to that bit.

I put a note of iron into my voice. 'We will not have time to stop at the fountain, because we will *still* be walking past the Pantheon and the Piazza Navona. We will go past, but *not* inside, the Vatican Museum and the Janiculum. After ducking the pigeons in Saint Peter's Square, we walk faster past the Catacombs . . .'

'*Past* the Catacombs?' moans a disappointed voice.

'*Past* the Catacombs,' I insist. 'And the via Appia Antica *and* the Basilica of Saint Paul *and* the Gallery of Borghese *and* the famous Museum of Roman Civilisation.'

I pause. The silence is so intense that we can hear, outside through the pouring rain, the merry clash and clatter as Rome's motorists try and prove their driving is better than the next man. It's all a virility thing. They have small cars, but long radio aerials!

'Any questions?' It's like a regimental sergeant-major asking if there are any complaints about the cookhouse food.

'Right. That's this morning. But this afternoon we will really hit the highspots. There is a choice. You can either see the Street of the Soapmakers, or the Street of the Chairmakers. Tonight there will be organised games of Happy Families.'

Having delivered all this, I can stand back and admire my own skill. To say they look unhappy is true as far as it goes, but it doesn't go far enough. I did once see a bloke who was more miserable. A street-sweeper in Birmingham called Lance Boyle. He'd just done his patch for the day when round the corner came the Royal Canadian Mounted Police on a courtesy visit.

Told who they were, afterwards, he is reported to have said: 'If they're so effing good at getting their effing man then they can effing clean up their own effing manure.' Of course he didn't say 'manure'.

'What's the matter? You don't look all that happy with the efforts that Colt Tours have made on your behalf.'

A bald, rather unctuous young man named Harold Gorringer coughs nervously. 'Pardon me, Mr ... Mr.'

'May.'

He looks confused. 'May what?'

Well, it's been a long time since we had that one; I didn't want you to think that I'd forgotten it.

'Jonathan May,' I say, smiling encouragingly.

'Yes. Well, all these things you've planned. I mean, I know they're included in the price and all that, but are they actually ... you, I mean, compulsory?'

I stagger back, clapping my hands to my brow as though someone has slipped a ferret inside my trousers. Careful, Jonny. Mustn't overdo it.

'Well, Mr Gorringer. No, I suppose they're not actually compulsory. Why, did some of you want to go about and do your own things?'

Glances are exchanged. I press home my advantage. Always a good thing to do. I mean to say: All's fair in love and love.

'You mean some of you would rather go to excellent eating-places, or wander round the wonderful museums and art galleries? Go shopping in some of the best boutiques and markets in all Europe? Eat, drink and be merry? Feel the freedom that is the right of all holidaymakers? How can that be?'

Have I gone too far? I see traces of guilt on one or two faces. No, all is well. One by one, then in groups, they all flock up and mutter how, if I don't mind, they'd like to go off and potter about on their own. Perhaps in other cities . . .

'Of course, of course,' I say, as understanding as the best family doctor. The lobby empties, and I am about to rush up the stairs to leap back into the sack with Mrs J. when I feel a tug at my sleeve. It is the execrable Gorringer, with his toothless parent in tow.

'Pardon me, Mr May. My mother and I will be going off on our own, but she would like to play in the Happy Families contest tonight. Is that all right?' And he grins at me.

Obviously he's joking. Nobody could be that foolish. I smile back. 'Of course. My room at seven. Look forward to seeing her there. Goodbye. Must rush. Don't want to miss the picturesque ruins of the stables off the via Fellini. Sure you don't want to . . .?'

They have gone, with the old lady showing a surprising turn of speed for such age.

If ever there was a walking advert for compulsory euthanasia it is Mother Gorringer. A couple of hundred years ago she'd have been one of the first for the ducking stool. I swear I have seen flowers wilt as her shadow falls across them.

I take the three flights of stairs in one leap, all tiredness gone. The old hot rod is ready for the banger special and I slip into my cupboard – sorry, room – for a wash and a second shave. Elizabeth is fussy about getting scratches on her tender cheeks.

Aaah. Caught you out in a naughty thought there, didn't I? Which cheeks? you wondered. I'm not going to tell you. Try and get to the bottom of it.

Whoops!

The morning goes by in a haze of melting flesh and soft embraces. If they filmed it, they'd keep cutting away to us walking through a rippling field of poppies while some warm-voiced country singer, like Kris Kristofferson or John Stewart, provides gentle music.

It really is a nice time.

We get up and shower – it's an infallible rule of the travel business that if there's a bad room going, it's the poor bleeding courier who gets it. He's less likely to complain. So Liz has a shower in her room.

We have a nice lunch in a quiet restaurant only a few yards from the hotel. It's still raining.

I have the Fettucine and Liz tries the Abbachio. You didn't know I was an international gourmet, did you? I'm not. The waiter takes us for a honeymoon couple – which nearly puts me off the food – and insists that we have the best. Rather a lot of cheese and garlic for my tastes, but he is a very big waiter and I don't like the way he keeps sharpening a huge carving knife. A bottle of chianti gets us ready for the afternoon session and we totter back to the hotel room, and . . .

Fall asleep. It's been a hard day and night, and I start sleeping like a log. It must be all that working like a dog they talk about. Liz dozes off as well and we don't come round until after five.

What a waste of a day in Rome! Still it's not entirely wasted. I've caught up on some of my kip and Edgar enjoyed it. He wouldn't really have liked the via Lamborghini anyway.

I am dreaming about having this silver screw right through the middle of my navel. I see doctors all over the world, and none of them can do anything to help me. Finally, in desperation, I go to this old faith-healer. He looks at it, throws a puff of green powder on his brazier and tells me to go home, and put my bed in the moonlight so that the forces of good can work on this devilish screw and remove it. I thank him for it and rush home. Push my bed into the moonlight and go to sleep. When I wake up, the screw's gone. After all these years. I jump out of bed . . . and my bottom falls off.

At this moment I am awakened by someone knock, knock, knocking on Edgar's door. He rises to the occasion, while I get to grips with two mounds of whipped cream topped with cherries.

That's a bit of poetic licence. One pound fifty a year from all sub-post offices. And watch out, the poetic detector vans will be round your way soon.

The waves pound on the beach for the second time that day and we both roar through the chequered flag side by side. While we're relaxing I order dinner for two, but I have it sent up to my room to avoid any embarrassment for Elizabeth. She has to stay in the hotel for another couple of nights, while we'll be away by midnight.

I get dressed quickly and tell her the amusing anecdote about how boring old Gorringer and his mother turned out to have quite a sense of humour after all, with their joke about the mum wanting to play Happy Families.

Steak and salad shouldn't take long to ruin, so I kiss Liz a fond farewell. Au revoir really, since I'll be back in two turns of a tadpole's tinkle with a tray of supper.

The corridor is empty and I make my dash for my own room. I'm nearly there when I hear someone pattering along towards me. I duck into a bathroom and wait it out. The shower curtain has some nasty stains on it and I begin thinking about 'Psycho' again.

The cold tap suddenly coughs and spits out a jet of brown rust, nearly making me leap out of my espadrilles. The feet go past again and I relax. Of course. It's the waiter with the food. Then I hear more feet – high-heeled shoes clicking past, towards my room.

A smile edges nervously back. Elizabeth trying to give me a surprise. I'll surprise her. In the corridor again, I quietly open my door. It's half-dark and I can see a figure sitting by the bed, tucking into the steak.

'Now you're for it!' I yell, beginning to unzip my trousers.

The figure turns round. Dimly, through a dreadful fog, I hear a voice thanking me for the meal. Apologising for being a bit early.

Zipping up Edgar again, I close the bedroom door with a slow, inevitable fatalism.

Sod's Law playing its worst trick yet.

We get away from Rome on schedule.

If anyone, anywhere, anytime, asks me if I've got Mr Plod the Policeman, I shall die.

Just die.

CHAPTER SEVEN

We're in Zurich, and the sun is shining for the first time since we left London. It seems weeks ago. The horrors – and the highlights – of Rome are a dim memory. The coach trip is not the best fun in the world. Jonathan, as some of you will have noted, is not the traveller most likely to succeed. In not being travel-sick.

The first leg of the journey isn't too bad, with Liz to keep me occupied. My old man often says that I keep all my brains down in my pendulum and chimes. With nothing to distract my mind (?) the trip up from Rome to Switzerland is torture. Sick transit!

I reckon that the worst part of being travel-sick is the social embarrassment. People will just avert their eyes while you actually throw up and then press you with comments designed to help you feel better.

Comments like: 'Oooh, you do look queer.' 'All the colour's left your cheeks.' 'Do you know that there's sweat trickling down your face?' Or they show a shocking insensitivity to your condition. See a pregnant lady, and most (well, some) folks will help her to a chair. But one of the younger men in the party – in my illness I only guess that it's the one who's the wizard with women – sits next to me as I feel at my lowest.

In fact I'm actually trying to remember when I felt worse. There was the time that I . . . no, I don't think that I can tell you that. It was one of the most embarrassing things ever.

Let's change the subject. Although if I'm telling you the whole truth, as I am, then I suppose this'd better come out as well. My mum wouldn't go to visit a nudist camp, because she said she didn't want to let it all hang out!

Although you wouldn't think it now, I used to be quite good at sports. I was with the school team, going in a coach to an away fixture. Blazing hot day. Real scorcher it was.

Brand-new coach. Sparkling in the summer sun.

About twenty miles out I get the familiar cold sweat, and I know I'm going to be sick. Like I say, I hate the public side of travel sickness, so I go and sit on my own up the front of the coach. Most people are near the back, taking advantage of having the windows open jetting cool air on them.

Very discreetly, I throw up carefully into a hankie. Once it's done I don't feel too bad, and I'm quite chuffed nobody has noticed. I fold the handkerchief up into a tight ball and heave it out of the window.

So much for my hopes. The edge of the hankie gets caught in the corner of the open window and Swiiiiiiiiiiioooooooosh! All the way along the side of the coach. In all the windows. Covers everybody.

Still makes me blush, the horror of it all. I'll never forget the look on the driver's face when we finally stop. Like Wily Coyote as he realises that the vast boulder is about to fall back on his head and not drop on Road Runner. And 'Beep, beep' to you too!

This young fellow who's sitting next to me in the coach on the way to Zurich cheers my illness with a jolly story. It seems a friend of his has the trick on planes of taking a plastic bag of Russian salad in his pocket. He sits next to the most nervous person he can find, and keeps up a running commentary on how worried he is about being sick.

As soon as they're up, up and away, this fellow would start retching for the sky and pretend to be sick into the brown paper bag. His neighbour would look away, and then he'd quickly tip the Russian salad in the bag, and put it on the floor by his feet.

They go on a few hundred more terror-stricken miles and then this revolting man would ask for a spoon from the air hostess, pick up the bag and eat his Russian salad with every evidence of pleasure.

Collapse of neighbour.

Collapse of me when I hear the story.

Amazingly, I find his tale quite funny, and it really does make me feel better. I can actually look out of the coach windows and enjoy the trip. Particularly as Hugh James

David Thomas has finally mastered the idea of driving on the right-hand side of the road.

We crossed the border from Italy near Como a couple of hours back, and are not far from our destination. The mountains glisten in the rising sun like cake icing. The streams bubble like champagne. The roofs on the houses are thick and dull brown, like slabs of marzipan.

It's the only country I've ever visited that looks like a vast wedding reception.

I find it difficult to believe that I am really in Switzerland. Must remember to send a card to Linda and to my mum and dad. They've never been further than Llangollen, and they thought they'd need passports to get *there*.

Most of my clients have dozed along the way, and I have no need either to start them singing or, in some cases, to stop them. The good ship Venus never set sail, and Sir Jasper slept undisturbed.

The hotel isn't too bad. I doubt if the A.A. would even give it one star for trying, but not everybody wants to stay at an Alcoholics Anonymous hotel, anyway.

I wait around while all the guests bustle up to their rooms to settle down for a morning's sleep, ready for the afternoon's festivities. The prospect of a few hours in the sack is very attractive. The way things are going, I reckon I shall be a wreck by the time we get back to London. After what Liz said about the tour, I have been doing some hard thinking. It does seem oddly planned, even by the low standards of Rupert Colt Enterprises. Vast amounts of travelling to a rather peculiar selection of cities.

Still, none of the customers seems worried. Apart from Madame Gorringer, and she's the sort of woman who'd get in through the Pearly Gates (personally, I doubt her chances of rising rather than falling) and immediately start complaining that her harp isn't properly tuned.

There was that odd little man who kept hanging round the back of the coach when it arrived at Rome. Had a big suitcase and spent a long time talking with Hugh James David Thomas. Perhaps there is more in this package than meets the eye. I shall keep my eyes skinned. (Ugh!)

I am on the verge – which is neatly-mown grass, outside the hotel – when someone plucks me by the sleeve. A nasty-looking wizened plucker. I suspect he might be one of the famous gnomes of Zurich, offering to show me some filthy bank accounts.

Bed beckons, and I try to shrug him off, but his fingers are locked more tightly than my mum's round her bingo winnings.

'Eff off, smiley,' I say, with that famous May grin.

No response. His eyes look uncannily like oysters with a dash of tomato sauce and they roll knowingly at me.

'You are le chef of Colts?'

I wonder what's cooking, with a question like that. He sees that I am puzzled.

'You are the leader of these people?'

Obviously someone has told him to ask to be taken to the leader. I nod, hoping it's not another bad debt.

'Your name is . . .?'

'May.'

'May quoi?'

This is a Euro-joke, registered at Brussels under the Edict of Nantes. For those of you without basic French, I can see I have to explain that 'quoi?' is the French way of saying 'what?'. Yes, I know it's the same old joke again.

'My name is Jonathan May, and this is my guest party. Who are you?'

He is peering at a scrap of paper in his hand, trying to read some faint pencilled words.

'I am called Kart. Orson Kart. But you say your name is *Jonathan* May?'

'Yes,' I say, confused by him putting the Orson before the Kart.

'Oh, a million excuses. It is Monsieur Thomas that I wish to meet.'

He raises his trilby and slouches off through the slush.

Funny? I think. Thomas sees him talking to me and hurries after him. They walk down the street arm in arm, conversing animatedly.

If it weren't for the lure of the wooden steps to Bedfordshire and a soft pillow, I would press the matter further The one thing my old man taught me is to keep my nose clean. The best way of doing that is to keep right out of anyone else's business. Maybe Rupert is using Hugh James as a foil in some game. I bet its not cricket. The only cricket Hugh knows involves bowling maidens over.

There is a shattering noise behind me. The only comparison I can make is with a hundred elephants all breaking wind at the same moment. I rise several inches in the air, all thoughts of jiggery driven from my mind. Not to mention all thoughts of pokery.

My brochure tells me that the city is in the grip of the 'Sechselauten', which is a spring-time festival run by the guilds. The only guild I have ever come in contact with was on a young lady named Lily. Always suffering from a nasty cold, everyone would raise their glasses when Lily happened to be in the pink.

Anyway, this horrible noise subsides, and I risk a glance over my shoulder. There is a fat geezer in leather shorts and a beer gut bigger than my old man laughing fit to bust. Leaning on his shoulder is what I first think is a phallic symbol of stupendous proportions. Then I realise that it is an alpenhorn, with the accent on the horn.

Zurich's answer to Fred Emney obviously thinks it's a beezer wheeze to put the wind up innocent tourists. Nobody puts that much wind up Jonathan May and gets away with it.

I join the group of tourists admiring this hideous instrument, and under the guise of peering at the carvings, I spill some lighter fuel in the big end. A quick flash – with the lighter! – and there is soon a rewarding glow in the opening.

Pleased by the reception his act has got, he gathers his wind for another big puff. Which reminds me; I must send a card to Rupert.

The Swiss buffoon inflates his cheeks and sends a gale blasting down his alpenhorn. It is all my little fire needs to help it grow. Smoke billows out in a dense cloud, with the smell of burning cheese. I don't know why, but that's what it reminds me off.

He drops it and begins to run round in ever-decreasing

circles, screaming for help at the top of his voice. Don Goodall, I think it is, comes out of the hotel, sees what is happening and makes a suggestion of how to put out the fire, which would be very rude if it weren't so funny.

I am disappointed when a gendarme, or whatever they're called, appears and puts out the blaze with a couple of handfuls of snow. It melts.

I melt quietly into the hotel and go to my rest. I didn't know I had the famous Saint staying next to me. Or James Bond as he is now known.

How do I know who's there? All during my rest I keep getting disturbed by a woman's voice crying out: 'Oh, Roger... More... Roger... More...!!!!!'

I nip into the hotel restaurant for a quick one before retiring. Here is a tip. Please, no giggling in the back row there! If you go to Zurich, make sure your false teeth are firmly fixed in before ordering a meal.

I have a sort of Lancashire hot-pot of meat and vegetables with rice. Sounds nice. It is. Only trouble is telling the waiter what I want. It is called (the meal, not the waiter) Geshnetzeltes nach Zucher Art. After three attempts I wipe my mouth dry and simply point.

The waiter writes down 'Number 45'. Always eager to prove my foreign tongues, I ask him how you pronounce it.

''ow would I know. I only bin 'ere free days meself, ain't I?'

So much for glamour.

I reckon I am on safe ground when it comes to the booze. Prune liquor sounds a bit different. Appropriate too, as I have been having a little trouble in even passing the time. The wine waiter is a different kettle of fish. Even a horse of a different colour.

He hands me the wine list and I find the prune brandy I've heard about. I aim to make a hit with the Swiss. Here goes. By the hickory daiquiri! How do you pronounce 'Pflumli'? I try six times, my tongue getting more and more locked behind my teeth each time. The nearest I get sounds like

'Fumbly'. The waiter is getting impatient, clicking his biro meaningfully at me.

'Er . . . Coca Cola, please.'

Well, it is the real thing.

The waiter sniffs as though I'm something he's dredged up from the bottom of the last cask of Amontillado (for the love of God!).

Not a hit with the Swiss. More of a Swiss miss.

There is a local guide in Zurich who is employed on a miserly retainer by Colt Enterprises Limited, in a generous attempt to give the courier a bit of time off. The only thing Colt couriers ever need time off for is to catch up on their sleep because of the absurd schedules.

He comes round to see me before I pop into the land of Nod. He is four feet tall and his name is Matthew Horn. Rupert has warned me that he has a liking for the ladies and is known on the package-tour circuit as Horny Matt.

The English as she is mangled by Matt is not easy to reproduce. So I'm not going to try and reproduce it. He sounds like Doctor Kissinger with a *very* bad cold.

I ask him what he's planned for the day in Zurich. (Actually, it's now hissing down with sleet.) My plans include a lot of sleep. Followed by some shut-eye. Then forty or fifty winks. Followed, maybe, by some sleep.

Horn looks at me with eyes as limpid and trusting as a hungry crocodile. 'In the morning we will do the shops. In the lunchtime we will do the dipping. In the later afternoon we will do the burning of the Boog.'

Now the shopping I can understand.

'What is the dipping?' I dread his reply.

'You get things nice and warm, then you prepare what is to be dipped, making sure you take something firm. There is nothing worse than trying the dipping with something that is limp and soggy.'

Please! Stop that sniggering.

'Then you stir up the dipper in the thing, which is now hot and bubbling and ready. Then, when the end is all

93

covered with the thick liquid, you thrust it into your mouth and suck for all she is worth.'

Boggle, boggle goes my mind. What strange mid-European perversion can this be? Should I trust my passengers to this crazed person?

Horn sees the way I am looking at him and recoils a pace. 'What is wrong, Herr May?'

I fear I am trapped with a maddened deviate, and I look about me for another exit. There is none, and the only door out is so close that I would have to go close round the Horn to get to it. I decide to try calm reason.

'What're you on about?' I squeak.

'Fondue.'

'What?'

'Fondue. Fondue.'

'All fall down,' I mutter, inappropriately.

But the pfennig has dropped. I have heard about fondue. It's the done thing on big housing estates to invite your friends to a fondue party, where you all sit round and have a communal dip. I hear it's even replaced wife-swapping in parts of Kent.

Come on, you know what I'm talking about. A pot of bubbling cheese and stuff and you stick your meat or whatever and dip it in the boiling sauce till it's cooked.

Sounds very uncomfortable to me. Still, at least I now know what little Horn is on about.

'What then is the burning of the Doog?' If it's some sort of ritual destruction of the great Derek Dougan I shall combat it with every muscle in my flabby body.

'Not the Doog, but the Boog. Now is the feast of what we call "Sechselauten". It is a pageant where we hold fairs and balls and dances and things. Do you not hold balls in England, Herr May?'

'Not me personally,' I explain, wondering if this is one of Rupert's secret friends.

'Aah. Well, we fill up a big man made of cotton wool to look like an ice warrior ...'

'Snowman,' I interrupt. 'Ice warriors are only in Doctor Who.'

'What?'

'No, Who.'

'Where?'

'No, not where. Who.'

By now it is Horn's turn to back away, looking affrighted. He decides that cowardice is the best part of survival, and goes on about the Boog.

'This giant is also filled with bangs and all is set on fire. It is very jolly.'

It sounds as much fun as a weekend in a Billingsgate deep-freeze, but I suppose some people might like it.

'And you will do all this yourself without any aid from me?'

He beams. 'Yes. Yes, I will. You will be a back-number. Obsolete. Pouffff!' He accompanies the last word with a vague gesture to the sky.

I think he means that I will be needed like a spare chick at a poultry farmer's wedding. At least I hope that's what he means.

Waving a cheery farewell, Matt Horn vanishes out of the hotel. Two and a half seconds later I'm undressed and in between the cool cotton sheets. I need sleep so badly, you would not believe. There is nothing now going to stop me having a good twenty hours' uninterrupted kip. The 'Do Not Disturb' sign is on the door.

It is eleven thirteen in the morning. The next bulletin will be at about ten o'clock tomorrow morning.

Good night all. And remember, if you're on a bike, wear white.

BOOOOOOOOOOOOOOOOOOOOOOOOOOOOOOONG!

Ortega y Gusset! What in the name of Iscariot was that infernal noise? The end of the world is at hand. Must be. That was the Last Trump. (Seven of spades if you play bridge at all.)

Bleary-eyed, I sit up and peer suspiciously at my watch.

Eleven sixteen. But which day? I don't feel as though I've just snored through a whole day.

I decide it must have been some sort of traffic noise that jarred my sleep. Being disturbed like that when I'm asleep always makes me want to go all Welsh. You know; take a leak!

My tiny tinkle over, I topple back into the bed and prepare myself for slumber. A last look at my watch. Just three minutes before half-past eleven.

Good night all. Remember, a clown at the circus is real funny; on the highway he's a killer. And a road accident doesn't decide who's right; just who's left. And, leave your blood at the local blood-bank; not on the highway. This is Broderick Crawford saying 'ten-four' and see you next week.

Sorry, got carried away.

(Publisher's Note: We should be so lucky!)

Good night.

BOOOOOOOOOOOOOOOOOOOOOOOOOOOOOOONG!
BOOOOOOOOOOOOOOOOOOOOOOOOOOOOOOONG!

Hell's Bells!! Or, to be more accurate, the bells of the Sacristy of the Church of the Blessed Saint Bubo of Ishmaelia. The belfry is situated just across the courtyard from my room, and is driving me bats. Every quarter of an hour it chimes out. One of those very deep notes that seems as though they're loosening the fillings in your teeth.

The manager is very sorry. The bells stop at midnight and don't start again until five thirty in the morning. The news does not rouse me to give three rousing cheers. Not even one cheer.

With the aid of hunks of cotton wool and several pillows piled over my head (which makes me feel like the little princes in the Tower) I finally stagger over the finish line into slumber.

My last coherent thoughts are what I'd like to do to the

damnable Colt. I don't mind most of his stupid mistakes, but this is one clanger I could have done without.

At last I feel a new man. Considering what bad shape the old one was in, it is a miracle worthy of attention in the Vatican.

I ring round a couple of rooms, but everyone is still out shopping. My stomach feels less than full and I ring down for a bite of lunch.

Very efficient these Swiss. About ten minutes later and a man brings in a tray groaning with the weight of food on it. This is the way to live. The only thing that surprises me is that the tray is brought by a man rather than the girl who serves on this floor.

'Where is the chambermaid?' I ask.

The man looks surprised at the question. 'Ze washbasin is made in your own Stoke, and I zink ze chamber iss made there also.'

What a funny man. If he had a bit more brain he could grow up to be a half-wit.

I don't make a public appearance until after the others have finished their dipping. They come out of the fondue room looking like refugees from an action painting.

There is cheese on their cheeks, noses, in their hair, on their shirts and blouses, all over their trousers and skirts, and one young man, whose name is not a hundred miles away from Gorringer, even has strings of melted cheese all over his expensive rope sandals.

I wish I had a camera so that I could ask them to pose and say 'Cheddar'.

While they go up to change ready for the heady delights of the afternoon burning the Boog and aprés-skiiiiiing all over the place, I stroll out to look over the coach.

There is a rump sticking out of the boot. A petty thief, I think, and place a boot in the rump. It straightens up with a cry of surprise revealing the moustached face of Hugh James David Thomas.

'It's Hugh,' I say.

'Of course it's me,' he snaps back with a touch of the old acid.

'No, not "you". "Hugh",' I say trying to explain the situation.

'I know my own name. As well as you.'

'As well as Hugh what?' By now I am getting that aching feeling at the back of the brain that I get when someone tries to explain liquidity or quadratic equations.

'I may be Hugh . . .'

'And I may be May,' I interrupt amusingly.

For a moment I think he's going to lay one on the Jonny jawbone. As opposed to the jawbone of an ass.

(Publisher's Note: No comment!)

'You're May and I'm Hugh. Now what do you want?'

'I know you are Hugh. Oh, forget it. I just came out for a walk in the fresh air.'

I realise that Hugh is not at his jolly best, and seems a bit worried over something. As I come out of the hotel I think I see him shoving a polished wooden box into the boot.

'Souvenirs?' I ask. Just for something to say.

'What?' His eyes have narrowed suspiciously, like my mum's the first time she found a French letter in my jacket pocket. I told her it was a free offer with a bottle of Lucozade. She'd believe anything, my mum.

'That box.'

He stands back, revealing an empty box. Not even Long John Silver's left boot was any emptier.

I open my mouth to say something, then think better of it. There is definitely something going on around this trip, and I suspect that Rupert Colt is near the bottom.

Isn't he always?

While my clients enjoy their festival, I take Swiss leave and stroll round Zurich. This is the way to live. Unfortunately my salary isn't paid until I get back to London, so I'm short of the ready and do all my shopping from the outside of the windows.

There's one shop that's packed with specimens of the watchmaker's art. It reminds me of something I once saw in

98

a film I think its 'The Third Man' – the one with all that jingly zither music.

This bloke Harry Lime, played by Orson Welles, is up on this big wheel in the middle of Vienna, just after the war. Don't worry, this story does get us back to Switzerland.

He's talking about how all the warlike nations have made the greatest inventions. Then he says something like: 'In seven hundred years of peace and brotherly love the Swiss have only produced the cuckoo clock.'

There. Wasn't that interesting and appropriate? Well, appropriate then.

In some ways I find it hard to believe that it's really me, Jonathan May, standing here in the middle of Zurich in Switzerland. I mean, it's a foreign country. You know the feeling I mean?

7 April. David Frost and William Wordsworth. What would they have talked about if they'd ever met? How *super* the daffodils looked?

Our time in Zurich is drawing to a close. I can hear the crackle of fireworks going off somewhere on the other side of the city. Either that or the Zurich Godfather has just made someone an offer he couldn't refuse. Which is better than a dustman I used to know. He had a sideline selling off odd bits of rubbish he found in bins. He got very angry when he had a day when there was only refuse he couldn't offer.

My feet lead me back towards the hotel. It's still cold, and Edgar has withdrawn into his shell in protest at the wind whistling through my zip. I wonder how Liz is getting on in Rome.

I shiver suddenly at the chill of the early morning.

By the hotel most of my charges are back safely, though many are, as they say, a trifle over-emotional. Old mother Gorringer has had a right skinful and lunges at me attempting to plant a wet kiss on my youthful face. Talk about 'Has anyone got Mrs. Dracula the vampire?'

The sight of her open mouth reminds me of a nasty accident I once saw in a circus. This lion-tamer was doing his putting his head in the beast's jaws trick. Looking back on it,

I guess the clown really regretted bursting that balloon at just that moment.

The lion it was that panicked, but it was the man who really lost his head.

It's starting to snow a bit as we all pack into the coach, ready for the unbelievably long trek to Amsterdam. The winding Swiss roads are glistening with ice, and Hugh James David Thomas performs with masterly skill. By that I mean he avoids actually driving right off the road. Being in a coach steered by Thomas is hours of boredom broken into by moments of stark terror.

Already I am getting home-sick. I don't think I'm really cut out to be a travelling man. I yearn for the clammy streets of Britain. I yearn for my little pad in Bacon Hill. Not to mention the loving arms – and other things – of Miss Loveband in said flat.

I get a lump in my throat thinking of Linda Loveband. Deep in my throat.

I'm not sure I'm that keen on all these bleeding great mountains scattered all over the place. Very untidy it is, as well.

Already heads are nodding in the rows of seats in front of me. Once I can get off to sleep, I'm fine, but it's actually getting my eyes to close and stay closed that I find hard.

I check that I've got all the passports ready for presentation when we reach the frontier. Idly I glance through the pictures. Well, I am feeling a bit depressed so this is the ideal thing to cheer me up.

One that I let fall open on my lap has a grinning young man in it who resembles a drunken Indian princeling. His eyes have a glint to them that are as mad as a hatter's. The light in the coach is not that bright and it's hard to make out some of the faces. But this one really is a cilla. Sorry, that should be lulu.

Who can it be? I open the front and . . . yes, folks, you've guessed it. The name is Jonathan May.

As the white peaks whirl by us I am reminded of an old jest. It concerns Switzerland and her mountains.

It seems . . . all the best jokes begin with 'it seems' . . .

that a rather lecherous young man – let us call him 'Laurence' – visits Switzerland for the first time and stays with a certain Herr Softwinkel, who has three lovely young daughters and a rather attractive wife as well.

But Herr Softwinkel is a boor and a tyrant, who allows his family no freedom at all. He visits a house of ill-repute in the hamlet where they live but would never consider allowing his wife or daughters any sort of sexual liberty.

One day Laurence and Softwinkel go for a tramp in the mountains. But the tramp gets away. No, that's another joke. While they hike over the peaks, they hear 'Yodeladeeoo, yodeladeeoo' floating over the snow.

'What is that?' asks young and handsome Laurence.

'That is yodelling,' grunts the surly and unattractive Softwinkel. 'It is the way we communicate over vast distances. I am good at it.' And he demonstrates. 'Yodeladeeoo. Yodeladeeoo.'

The echoes bounce back off the glaciers.

Laurence practises yodelling and also becomes quite good at it. Then, on the last day of his visit, Herr Softwinkel comes home and finds his first daughter sighing in ecstasy by the gate, her clothes in ribbons. In answer to his shouts, she only smiles and mutters 'Laurence'.

By the front door is daughter two, in a similar state. By the back door is daughter three. Her underclothes dangling from the door-knob, a smile of delight still on her cheeks.

Herr Softwinkel rages off in pursuit of the rogue, shotgun in hand. But Laurence has too long a start (among other things.)

Finally, he catches a glimpse of him, miles away across a great canyon. Safe and away. Softwinkel yells across at him: 'Yodeladeeoo! You've made love to all of my daughters!!!!'

Faint, floating over the icy space, he hears: 'Andyouroldladytoo!!'

I bet it rains in Amsterdam. Still, helps them grow their bleeding tulips.

CHAPTER EIGHT

It's raining when we get to Amsterdam. Still, I suppose it helps them grow their bleeding tulips.

The trip across Europe has been a barrel of laughs. Everyone has been constantly cheerful and totally uncomplaining, merely marvelling at the passing panorama. I have had no trouble with any of them, and the lovely Gorringers have been particular fun to be with.

I suppose among my millions of avid readers there will be someone who believes that last paragraph. So, for the benefit of that person, I will make it clear that I am being sarcastic for dramatic effect. In fact it is hour after hour after hour after hour of hell and torture. You would not believe some of the moans.

One man wants to know when we will be getting to Madrid. It has taken him six days to suss out that he isn't actually on the right coach. Maybe there are thousands of people who do that every year. Doomed to wander forever across the coach-routes of Europe.

But, at last, here we are. I look around for the local guide that my much-folded itinerary tells me should be here to greet us. All I can see is a fat little man in tight orange trousers, lime-green windcheater carrying a silver and gold golfing umbrella. And I'm sure that he's not...

Yes.

He is.

'Hello, dearie. Rupert told me to get in touch as soon as you landed, so to speak. I must say I don't mind getting in touch with a nice boy like you. What's your name, love? Thompson, or something like that, isn't it?'

Aha. So this gay fellow thinks I'm Thomas, and since I think that Thomas is a contact man for some sort of game that Rupert is playing and since I want to find out about

Rupert's tricks, then I'll pretend that I *am* Thomas and then this man will tell me what he's supposed to tell Thomas and . . .

'I'm Thomas.'

Brighton and Hove Albion! ! ! By the time I'd worked out what I was going to do, the real Hugh James David Thomas has got out of his cab and come round to join us.

'Oh!' chirps Mr. Purple Trousers. 'Then who's this?'

'He's May.'

'Ooooh. May as in West?'

I laugh. Well, if you'd heard the same joke about your name thousands of times, you might find it funny to hear a new one.

What do you mean? You have and you don't? Cheek!

'I'm Jonathan May. I'm the courier.'

'Good for you. Make a career of courier and you won't go far wrong. My name is Winchester.'

'As in cathedral or as in gun?' I quip back at him.

He slaps me on the wrist. 'Willy Winchester, dearie. An old friend of Rupert Colt from way back, if you know what I mean?'

I reassure him that I do. He and Thomas can't wait to get away from me to discuss their business. I shake hands with Willy and retire.

From where I stand, I can only snatch an occasional word. 'Two gross . . . space for . . . customs . . . three grand if it's . . . commission.'

Then they go further out of earshot, and the wind and rain whip all the chat away. Shame, because it was a nice running conversation with that sort of crisp chat away.

(Author's Note: There is a concealed joke in that last sentence. Please re-read it with care. Thank you.)

I spin round, ready to climb back up the stairs to the hotel. For a horrifying second I think that I must have been stricken blind. The next thought is that someone has had the unamusing idea of creeping up behind me and thrusting two round scented cushions in my face. My third thought is the right one.

And the left one.

'I'm terribly sorry, Miss,' I stammer, unable to take my eyes off the biggest pair of bra-fillers it has ever been my good fortune to run into.

'That's all right. It was my fault.' She is not the giantess I at first thought. It was the fact that she was standing two steps higher than me that caused the pleasant juxtaposition of my peepers and her jeepers.

I stand aside to let her go past me, but she doesn't make any attempt to move. She is peering at my chest. Perhaps she is admiring my suit. Then I realise that she is reading the label pinned to my lapel. The lapel label says 'Colt's for Quality'.

He could get done under the Trade Descriptions for that.

'You are with Colt's?'

'Yes. I'm Jonathan May. That's my name.'

She smiles, and the sun shines. Actually it carries on pouring down, but the effect of her gleaming smile at such close quarters has the same effect as a blast of sunlight.

She is fairly tall; only an inch or so below my height, though she is wearing high-heeled clogs. Short blonde hair, framing a heart-shaped face. Blue eyes, brighter than my old man's at opening time.

'My name is Zondag. Marika Zondag. I am your helper. It is only a part-time job for me. I am a student, so I take many other kinds of work to help pay my way.'

I smile vaguely, hardly able to believe my good luck. The Amsterdam day is one where I don't really need a helper, as there is nothing planned, and the merry throng are free to go and do their own things where and how they want to. So this means that I will be free to let Marika Zondag show me her own sights.

'Are you married, Jonathan?'

'No!!! No!! No! No. Why?'

She shows me, lowering her head to mine, probing at my mouth with her soft tongue and warm lips. 'I am a moral girl, Jonathan. I will not go to bed with married men. Even if they are as nice as you are.'

Then her lips get busy again. I can hardly believe my

luck. I've heard about the free and easy life of the young in Amsterdam, but this is ridiculous.

Still hers are two lips from Amsterdam that I can't have enough of.

Somehow the tour party gets forgotten, and I find that I'm nowhere near as tired as I thought I was. She comes with me to my room, and has Edgar perking up before you can say 'Gillie, gillie, ossenfefferkatzennellenbogenbythesea'. Now please don't write to the publishers saying that I've got it all wrong.

I know. But it's near enough, and you know what I mean. Actually, Edgar perks up quite a long time before you could say that.

The sun has really come out – it's not the only thing – and a strip of pale yellow creeps round my room as Marika and I get together at cementing Anglo-Dutch relations. We make a good job of it, so we decide to do some recementing.

There's more mortar to this job than meets the eye, and there's not a single spare brick around. The time passes all too quickly. The one thing that I find a bit puzzling is the way that Marika keeps wanting to know how many times I can do this.

'What for? Are you auditioning me for a star part in a live sex show?' I ask, jokingly.

'Of course not; though there is good money to be made if there are two people who can do it well together.'

'Well, if we're ever short of money, then we know where to go.'

Marika Zondag is one of the most enthusiastic players of this rather specialised game that I've ever come across (I said 'across'). Poor Edgar is beginning to feel as though he's been through a mangle, backwards, and I'm forced to suggest that it might not be a bad idea if we call a halt for today, and pick up where we leave off tomorrow.

'Tomorrow is not Sunday?'

'No. Why?'

'Never on Sundays,' exclaims Miss Zondag. Rather confusingly.

It is agreed that I will now rest myself and Edgar, while she goes off home. Tomorrow morning I will call on her and we'll walk around Amsterdam and take in the sights and then, maybe, have a bit of . . . you know.

I must remember to buy a present for Linda Loveband. Maybe a hand-knitted Dutch cap.

We agree to meet on the corner of Kalverstraat at eleven. I sleep the sleep of the just. But only just. I have a recurrent dream in which Rupert Colt dressed as a big fairy keeps trying to catch me in a gauze net. He shouts out what he'll do to me with his wand if I don't stop poking my nose into his business. His business is one place I will try and keep my nose out of. But there's definitely something going on that is very fishy.

And I don't mean Iceland's two-hundred-mile limit!

I have had another quick shufti at the boot of the coach, and I am beginning to suspect that there may be some sort of secret compartment hidden at the back.

But Marika is waiting.

As it happens – guys and gals – I am early, so I wander to a newsstand and flip through some magazines.

By Screw and Suck! The shops in good old Soho are peddling infants' adventures compared with some of this stuff. I have never seen such detail. I have had some skinless sausages for my breakfast, and the sight of all these . . . spam syringes, brings it all back. Bleeding nearly brings it all back up.

There are titles like: 'Keep it in the Family', 'The Pig in the Middle', 'Lap-dogs', and so on and and on and on. My main thought is to wonder whether the animals included in so many of these magazines enjoy it any more than the stony-faced boys and girls.

If you could get hot stuff like these past the customs, you'd make a bomb in London. I don't go in for all that kind of scene – animals and lots of people all doing things to

106

each other at once. One day I will tell you about an orgy I attended. My main worry was not being able to concentrate and failing to keep my end up.

There isn't a clock in sight so I stop a friendly-looking bobby and ask him the time. He stares at me like I've threatened his grandmother with a rotting cucumber.

'You look to me like a degenerate hippie. Have you got your proof of identity and enough money to get you to the nearest frontier? If not, I shall be pleased to direct you to the canal so that you can wash your greasy hair and the lice-infected rags you are wearing.'

I am prepared to assume that this is the only miserable, bad-tempered sod in the whole Amsterdam police force, but why is it me who has to get him? Why couldn't I have got that nice Mr Van Der Valk? He'd probably have asked me back to his flat for a super meal. On second thoughts, he probably wouldn't.

He's dead. I read the book he dies in.

Hurriedly, I wander away from paranoid super-cop and am greatly relieved to see Marika running towards me. She looks smashing. Tight cotton blouse over lovely breasts. No bra. I mean, that stands out a mile. Striped cotton skirt and no tights.

Very summery. At long, long last it actually looks as though this courier business might not be such a dead-loss after all. She hugs me and squeezes my arm. Squeezes my thigh. Even Edgar finds things a bit of a squeeze.

'I thought we might go on a barge down the canal, Jonny. Then, this evening, we will stroll along and see some of the sights. Then, after that ...'

Edgar is becoming excited. It stands out a mile. Like her peaches. I know some writers describe them as melons, but I find that a bit ridiculous. Think about melons. Huge ungainly things. But, peaches. Firm and fresh. The sensation as you get your lips round them, and the juice trickles down your chin.

Funnily enough, she buys a bag of peaches and we nibble happily away on the boat. It has a glass roof, so that you can see all the lovely old buildings going by. Because it's still quite early for the tourist season, there aren't many others on board.

Marika is an excellent guide, and shows me things that I wouldn't have believed on a barge on a canal in the middle of Amsterdam. Admittedly, we're in a sort of cubicle at the back – sorry, stern – and there is a sort of privacy. The only problem there is this glass roof. Every time we go under a bridge, we stop the traffic.

Miss Zondag seems to enjoy the risk of detection and the rather public nature of our embraces. The trip is not cheap, but she pays her way, which helps out my diminishing resources. There is a lot to be said for going Dutch.

When we get to the end, she is having such a good time that she insists that we come all the way back again. Sort of double-Dutch, I suppose.

By now I fear that word of our exploits has spread and the bridges are lined for our return. Crowds of noisy urchins lean over and shout at us. I cannot believe that they are merely informing us of the score in the Test Match or wishing us a happy trip.

My guides notes says that one should not miss the raw herrings that are sold on street stalls with chopped onion. I only wish that I could have missed them. However, they have a way of making something of an impression on one. The city doesn't have a bad smell at all, but the herrings win by a nose.

Marika decides she wants something sustaining to keep her going through the evening. Although she's had her mouth full for most of the afternoon. I am greatly relieved that the next hop of Jonny May's Magical Mystery Tour is the shortest. To Paris. We don't have to leave until early next morning, so I can actually go out and enjoy something of the night life of Amsterdam. The next hop is also the last.

We arrive in Paris on 10 April. Have a couple of days in the romantic city and arrive back in London on the 13th. A Friday, I notice gloomily.

That evening Marika takes me to eat at a Chinese restaurant near the city centre. For a student struggling along on odd jobs she seems pretty flush to me. All the waiters know her and we are waved to one of the best tables in the place.

She is a lovely girl. She is still concerned about my health and keeps asking me if I feel up to it. Although it's nice to have someone so worried about you, there is something about her constant questions that begins to bother me.

'I did all right before, didn't I?' I ask, over the mixed vegetables.

'Yes, darling. Of course you did. That's what worries me. I don't want you to have tired yourself out before tonight.'

'No danger of that. As long as I can still raise a smile, worry not.'

She gives me her Grade-A beam. Full beam. 'Here, Jonny, why don't you have a little nibble on my dumplings? While nobody is looking.'

Has she no shame? Do I look the sort of fellow who would nibble on a lady's dumplings in a crowded restaurant? Unless, it suddenly occurs to me, Marika actually means that she wonders if I would like to nibble her . . . pork-filled little dumplings which she has ordered as her first course.

Sorry, folks. False alarm. She means dumplings as in food and not dumplings as in . . . chesty substances.

We chat a bit more over the various courses, with me exercising the famous, not to say notorious, May wit. I am somewhat put out when Marika fixes me with her glittering eye and says: 'Jonny. Are you getting sarkey?'

Now, I don't like sarcasm – specially when it's directed at me – and I tell her so in no uncertain terms.

'Jonny. I was not telling you off for being sarcastic. I was asking you to order the saki.'

I always try not to betray my ignorance over anything, so I call the waiter over and confidently ask for saki. He smiles and starts to shuffle off, when I have an afterthought. To show my knowledge of Chinese cuisine, I also order some special fried rice with this saki. Whatever it is. Sounds like some sort of fish.

The waiter and Marika both look puzzled. A few minutes

later he brings a plate of their special rice and a small jug of water and two glasses. I thank him and sit and wait for the saki.

'What are you waiting for, Jonny, and what do you want all that extra rice for?'

I grin knowingly, feeling sorry for her. Fancy not knowing how to act in a Chinese restaurant. I explain. 'The rice is to have with the saki, and that's what I'm waiting for. While I'm waiting, I'll have a sup of this water.'

She begins to laugh, and goes on laughing. I wonder whether my flies are open, but I haven't been feeling any unusual draughts round Edgar's front door. I ask her what's so funny.

'Oh, Jonny. Saki is a sort of Chinese wine. That's what's in the bottle. Tell the waiter to take the rice away. You won't be able to perform properly on a full stomach.'

'I'm not sure I'd call it performing, love. It's not as though we were going to give a public display.'

And I laugh. Loudly.

And she laughs. Hesitantly.

To cover what seems a slightly embarrassing moment, I take a slug of saki, and spit it out on the carpet. The waiter sees this and comes running up, looking concerned.

'What is long?' he asks.

There is an answer to that question, but I'm far too modest to give it.

'What?' I ask.

'What is long, sir. You no like saki?'

'Oh, what's *wrong*? Yes, it's this saki. It's warm. Take it away and bring me some fresh.'

Before he can reply, Marika interrupts me. 'Darling, saki is supposed to be drunk at blood heat.' And she waves the puzzled waiter away.

'Well, I reckon the bloke who cooked that was a bit too hot-blooded,' trying to save my face. Actually, saki is a long way from the top on my list of favourite drinks. I find it not unreminiscent of scented camel's pee.

No, as a matter of fact I haven't ever drunk scented

110

camel's pee. But, if I had, then I'm sure it would taste just like saki.

After we leave, Marika takes me for a stroll around Amsterdam. It's a bit like I imagine Venice to be. The sort of place where you take care where you're walking in case the road suddenly turns into a canal.

I have been making tactful enquiries about the naughty side of Amsterdam, and Marika responds by taking me by the arm (among other places) and leading me down by the Central Station, where there is what is called the Zeedijk district. It's a cross between Shepherd's Market and Soho. She tells me some amazing facts.

The Dutch have a strange, but oddly sensible, outlook on the ladies of the night. Technically, they're illegal. But they are all taxed about eighteen thousand guilders per year. Their prices aren't that high, so they have to get through a rapid turnover of clients. Marika has some friends who do this as a sort of part-time job, and she says some of them get through over twenty punters a day.

I read an article about this place in Germany where the tarts sit round in windows and you can take your pick. It's a bit like that in this part of Amsterdam, though there are also girls in the streets and even some riding up and down on bicycles, showing a truly amazing amount of leg.

It is only an occasional tug at my dangling pendant by Marika's little fingers that reminds me of where I am and who I'm with.

'No, Jonny. You may look and maybe after I'll introduce you to one or two of my friends. I'm sure they'd do you a special price.'

That's what comes of being in the holesale trade!

After a bit, all this window shopping gets hard on the feet, and Edgar is getting frustrated. It's like a soldier being given blank ammunition all the time. He wants to be up and doing. They like it up 'em, you know.

'Er, Marika.'

'What is it, Jonny?' pressing so hard against me that I can feel every muscle quivering. With a quiver like that, who needs Robin Hood?

111

'Isn't it about time, we . . . well, you know . . . went back to your place and . . .?'

She looks at her watch. 'No. It isn't quite time yet. I think in about another half hour we can go and get ready.'

There is something peculiar in the state of things here. Why is timing so crucial? Does she turn into a pumpkin at midnight? And, why do we have to get ready? I hope she's not one of those kinky birds you read about in certain family papers on a Sunday.' "I Could Only Do It In Diving-Suit" Says Mother of Four.' 'Night He Saw Divorcee's Unusual Wardrobe!'

I don't fancy that. I mean, clothes turn me on as much as the next man, but I go for sexy nighties and black stockings and naughty knickers and that sort of thing.

We go and have a cup of coffee in a little bistro, followed by a gin at a bar on the edge of the Zeedijk district, full of attractive young ladies with hard eyes and middle-aged men with swollen wallets and high hopes.

I see Marika still glancing at her watch, and I begin to get increasingly uneasy. We don't have *that* much time to waste and I want to be getting on with it.

She pours me a third gin, making some joke about putting lead in my pencil. If we go on much longer it'll need a pencil sharpener to get it into action.

At about ten she stands up and says: 'Right. *Now* we can go and get on with it. You're not nervous, are you, Jonny?'

'No. Why should I be? I have done it before, you know. You won't be having any of the old cherry-ripe with me, sweetheart.'

She seems as though she might say something, but then thinks better of it. We wind and wend our way through a maze of narrow streets. An amazing maze. It gets a bit misty, so there is a haze in the amazing maze. The gin is working well and I find I am in a bit of a daze in the haze in the amazing maze.

I try to gaze into . . . By Rack and Hook! I must stop that. There. It wasn't hard.

Through this warren of alleys, we finally come to a tiny

door set in a wall covered with advertisements for pepper-mints. The door coincides with the hole in the middle. Inside it is as dark as a cockroach's cavern. We climb up a flight of rickety steps, and through two more doors.

There is the smell of cigarette smoke and I can hear the faint hum of conversation, punctuated with bursts of cheer-ings. It doesn't sound all that far away.

'What's all that noise?'

I can't see Miss Zondag any more, but her hand is still clamped in the place that cheers. We seem to be in some sort of narrow corridor.

'Relax, darling. Trust Marika and lie back and enjoy it. It will be a new experience for you. Something to tell your grandchildren.'

If I have any! There is something about the set-up that makes me more and more uneasy. I wish I could put my finger on it.

Oooooooh!

'There, Jonny. You see how ready I am for you.'

I *have* put my finger on it!

She opens another door, and the noise seems louder. Like a crowd talking softly behind a plush curtain. The room is very dimly-lit, and I can just make out a bed in the middle of a bare expanse of floor. Although I don't see her do it, Marika must have switched on a hi-fi, as the 'Theme from Shaft' booms out.

How appropriate, I think.

Marika is by the bed, beckoning for me to go and sit by her. I stroll over, trying to keep my cool, although Edgar is all ready to spit defiance at the world.

I trip over a wire stretched across the floor and nearly squash the family heirlooms. To my disquiet, I think I can hear someone laughing at my stumble.

'Marika!' I hiss. 'There's someone here.'

By now she has her hand on mine, and she smiles. 'Don't be silly, Jonny. How could that be? Now, sit there while I get undressed.'

The thought of watching her peel off is enough for me to

temporarily forget my doubts. I flop on the bed, alarmed by the jingling of the springs.

I fear this is going to be yet another of those very tedious passages where I describe a young woman getting all of her clothes off. Move on a few paragraphs and you won't have to sit through it.

The music seems a little louder. And the light seems a little brighter. I reckon that anticipation must have made all of my senses that much keener.

Marika grins at me and begins to move sexily round the bed, peeling off her clothes in time to the beat . . . of the music. Her tight blouse and skirt soon fall into the darkness.

She wriggles out of her bra, cupping her breasts in both hands, and sort of offering them to me for inspection. If I were hungry, I would prefer melons, but they look fine for me at this particular moment. She lobs the bra into the outer blackness of the room.

I can swear I hear someone say 'Thank you'.

I sit up and swing my feet to the floor, intending to get to the bottom of things. Marika has the same idea and is peeling off her tights, leaving her only in a star-spangled pair of pants that would not win the approval of my mother. Her idea of a pair of knickers is something that begins well above the navel and ends well below the knee.

It *isn't* imagination. The music is louder, and the room is lighter. But it's only a central light over the bed that's getting stronger.

I stand up.

I sit down again.

Well, so would you if you'd just had a pair of frilly pants draped over your head, followed by a naked lady pushing you in the chest. Yes, you would.

That is, if you ever have the chance.

I flop backwards, while Marika sits on my chest and begins to rip off my trousers. I worry for the safety of Edgar under such rude treatment, but she is a well-built and very persuasive lady and I give up an unequal struggle. I am happy to lie back and admire the view. By now I can see I'm *really* getting to the bottom of things.

The trousers wing away and Edgar sniffs the air with all the uprightness of a Trafalgar Square Christmas tree.

There is a loud round of applause. I am a bit annoyed by it and am glad when a voice says: 'Quiet please, ladies and gentlemen. You'll put the performers off.'

'Quite right. It will put the . . .

Just a minute there, feller! Just a goshdarned minute!

I tap Marika on the most accessible part of her body, feeling a bit of an ass, and she turns round, looking worriedly over her shoulder. 'What's up, Jonny?'

'Apart from me, what's all this running commentary?'

'Oh, that. Ha, ha, ha.' She attempts a hollow laugh. 'That's the billiard hall directly underneath my place. It's a trick of the acoustics.'

Why, I hear many of you saying, doesn't he suss out what's going on? Can he really be taken in by such an obviously facile excuse?

Yes.

And so would you if you had an expert performer playing with your pipes. For some reason, it rapidly becomes less and less important about all these odd happenings.

The beef bazooka is ready, willing and, I hope, able. Marika rolls round into a more accessible position and I begin to play my part in the festivities. In a very few seconds my precious liner has come into port and is rocking gently in time to Isaac Hayes.

'Try and make it last,' she whispers in my ear.

Not the most tactful of things to say. It reminds me of the time that I am best man at a mate's wedding and his wife's mother stands behind me at the reception, constantly hissing: 'Make them laugh! Why don't you say something funny and make them laugh?'

Still, I do my best. Anyway, I reckon that a well-sustained performance over five thousand metres goes down better with the paying customers than a flashy dash over a hundred metres.

Marika Zondag may not do it on Sundays, but she makes up for that on other days of the week. The bed jingles and

115

jangles and the Shaft goes faster and faster. The light is becoming so bright that I have to close my eyes as we enter the last furlong.

Earth moves. Civilisations tumble. Explosions, bells, sirens and fire-crackers go off. There is a noise like air escaping from a punctured tyre, right in my left ear. It is only Marika indicating her pleasure.

Panting in short pants – I know I'd taken them off – I subside on the bed by the juddering figure of my little Dutch doll. The applause grows and swells.

'Someone must have potted a difficult red downstairs,' I say.

'You can say that again, Jonny dear,' grins Marika.

I stand up on the bed and shade my eyes, because it now seems possible to see beyond the stark light over the centre of the room.

And I see rows of men and women, all laughing and cheering and pointing at Edgar, who is a little limp after his exercise!!

There is a moment when I actually hope that I have gone crazy. Anything, rather than this shame.

There is a crackling as Isaac Hayes finishes his thing and a voice booms out, with a heavy Dutch accent.

'Thank you, ladies and gentlemen. A big hand for two such dedicated performers. All the way from Bulgaria; Sonia and Ivan. The next performance will be in half an hour. Until then, the Rupert Colt Canyon of Passion invites you into the next room where drinks are being served.'

'I'm sorry, Jonny. But I told you I needed the money, and I didn't think you'd agree if I told you first.'

That's one way of putting it. Still, I think, as I grab for a blanket to cover up my assets, I'll have something to tell my brother Morrie when I see him next.

He says you never get anywhere by lying down on the job.

Marika shares her cut with me – I should think so too – and the manager offers me a permanent position with him.

116

I'm tempted, until he says: 'And only six performances a day'.

There are limits for an artist like me.

And so, we say goodbye to Holland and head for the delights of Paris on the 10th. Last stop before home.

CHAPTER NINE

I once went to Paris for a day trip with the school. I'd been really looking forward to it. Eating frog's legs. Seeing the Eiffel Tower. The Louvre and the Mona Lisa. Not to mention all those ladies I'd seen in some of my old man's magazines that he used to keep at the bottom of his sock drawer. Ladies who wore skirts slit right up to their ears, with black fish-net stockings held up by garters.

I couldn't wait to get there. The previous night, for a dare, I'd eaten a half-dozen snails that a mate of mine had brought me. Said it would get me in the mood for Paris. They were horrible. Someone told me that you need a special kind of snail anyway.

These tasted like rejects from Fort Dunlop. And they didn't give me a flavour of Paris. They did give me one of the finest cases of the Mrs Dales (diarrhoea) I have ever had. From the moment I set foot in France to the moment I got back to Birmingham, I felt as though the world had dropped out of my bottom.

Still, this time things are going to be one whole lot different. On the coach Thomas gives me a bag of fondants someone had given him in Amsterdam. So he says.

I have a sweet tooth and they taste fine, although they seem to leave a slightly bitter taste in the mouth afterwards. Like watching Edward Heath on television.

History repeats itself, and so does my stomach. My head spins and my guts bounce up and down like a busy elevator. I manage to hold back the technicolor yawns that threaten to change the pattern on my room carpet, but I take to my bed and moan the night away.

I fear I am not the bravest of sufferers. I do not even have the sort of courage that enables men to eat a jam doughnut and never once lick the sugar off their lips. Surely the ultimate test of manhood.

Even as I toss and turn on my bed of pain – I suppose I

118

do exaggerate a bit now and again – I have lots of time to add two and two together. Despite my illness, I am still capable of coming up with the answer 'four' with disturbing frequency. Rupert is certainly up to something, or somebody. To my amazement, none of the party have made more than passing complaints to me about the oddly-scheduled tour. In their places I'd have been forced to complain. A tour de force, in fact. It occurs to me that all tours might be as awful as this one, but I dismiss the idea as being like the bucket of manure from Mongolia. Very far-fetched.

So, what is he up to? The odd packets in the boot make me suspect that Rupert must be smuggling. I hope it's not anything like drugs. I'm not one of those who shout out 'Don't Smoke on the Grass!' but there are other things for people to make a hash of. I must be getting old; I can remember when LSD meant money.

And the amiably lunatic Hugh James David Thomas must be in on it as Rupert's contact man. I wonder if they know that I'm on to them. I hope not. If they do, then they might... excuse me . . . I have to go and . . . you know, again. Back in a minute.

Ten minutes pass.

Aaah, that's much better. Using the bidet after reminds me of an unfortunate experience in Rome. One of the Beer-swiggers, or whatever they call themselves, found a bidet in his room.

You know what a bidet is! The thing in foreign bathrooms that sits there and grins up at you in the corner. Looking like a washbasin, only it's on the floor.

Well, this boozy bloke hadn't ever seen one before and he can only guess at what it's for. He guesses wrong. In the end he had to get a walking-stick to clean it out!

Now, where was I? Yes, thinking that if Rupert and his minions suspected that I was suspicious, then they might try to keep me out of circulation.

No. They'd never be able to do that. Unless they slipped me some kind of pill that would lay me on my back for the time we're in Paris and . . .!

The fondants! The bitter taste!!

By Hawley Harvey Crippen! I've been nobbled. Oddly, instead of making me feel worse, it brings out all the old May fighting spirit. No, I didn't really know there was any either. But there is, and I determine they won't get their evil way. I shall resist them with all the power and vitality and strength and vigour at my . . . Sorry, must just pop off to the bog again.

Four minutes later.

There, that didn't take so long. Fortunately, the May stomach is more hardwearing than most. You live as long with my mum's cooking as I did, and you'd have cast-iron guts as well. I've known her break a steel knife trying to slice one of her sponge cakes!

I get out of bed and commence a course of strengthening exercises. During these I observe a young girl in a bedroom across the courtyard, changing her clothes. What a lovely pair of . . . curtains . . . her room has. I can't take my eyes off them. Now she's doing some deep-breathing exercises and swinging to and fro. Goodness, how those . . . curtains move to and fro! What is she. . . ? Oh, she is taking off more of her clothes. What a well-upholstered . . . armchair . . . her room has. Such a nice shade of pink, with a little furry anti-macassar smack bang in the middle.

Holy mackerel! Deep-breathing *and* toe-touching! This is more than a man can stand. Well, my man is standing very well, thank you. And all in full view of any casual onlooker. Has she no shame?

I regret that I can describe no more as I slip and fall over. Slip off what? I hear you ask. You see, the chair that I've put on the table on the bed slips off and I topple to the carpet with a resounding tinkle.

A cold shower and I'm a new man. A great improvement on the old one, too. Sadly, the first day in Paris is shot to hell by the dreaded gut-rot they've foisted on me, but there are two more days to go. I shall sniff around to see what I can smell. Apart from garlic and Gauloises cigarettes, that is.

Though there is a tempting night's entertainment laid on by Colt's Tours, I take a rain-check on it and opt for a quiet night in my room. Just in case the young lady across the way feels active again, I get up every now and again to glance her way.

A light clicks on, and I can see a dim figure. Back turned to me. I manage to open my window and peer out, at great danger to life, limb and Edgar. It's taking off its jacket. Now the slacks are off. She's turning round.

Rupert would probably be in ecstasy, but beefy truck-drivers with hairy chests are not in my bag. No way. I climb between the sheets and go to sleep. Tomorrow is another day.

Tomorrow *is* another day. How true the old sayings are!

The sun shines and Paris is looking like it ought to, with the sun streaming off the boulevards and pretty girls everywhere. Somehow things always look different in the mornings and I have had a change of heart about Rupert and his games. I have decided that discretion is the better part of getting my salary paid and I'm not going to interfere.

Travel courier though I am – I *am* – I decide to spend a day sightseeing, and hop on the Metro. Although it's more or less the same as the London Underground, there's one big difference. Fewer British people and a lot more Americans. I sit opposite a tiny dwarf who is almost hidden behind a huge newspaper. I reckon he must be a Metro-gnome!

That joke brightens the day up even more and I stroll through Montmartre – which I always used to think was a sort of chocolate centre – with a song on my lips and pigeon crap in my hair. Since I sent a Dutch cap to Linda from Amsterdam, the least I can do is send a French letter from Paris, so I buy some notepaper and envelopes. I will write when I get back to the hotel tonight.

Lunch is a disappointment. I find an eaterie that advertises finest French cuisine. What they mean is finest French cuisine as practised in Minneapolis or Manchester. Onion soup that owes its origin to the famous cinquante-sept varieties. Hamburger and pommes frites made from potatoes (or pommes de terres as we linguists call them) that have been away from the fields for a very long time. Followed by a cream caramel that comes complete with its own exotic coating of dust.

The waiter holds his hand out for a tip and I press a centime into it. He looks down like he's found a caterpillar in his palm and says: 'Pardon, monsieur. But you have given me a centime for service.'

'Thank you for pointing that out, my jolly garçon,' I say, taking it back. 'An oversight on my part. I had intended to give you nothing.'

As I walk out, he seems to be making comments about my parenthood that would have my mum reaching for her rolling-pin. Excitable people, the French.

Back at the hotel, I have to put on my courier's hat and take those who want to go on a conducted tour of the famous Paris flea market. No, love, it doesn't mean a market where you can buy fleas. Though, it may well be a market where you can catch the little chaps, as some of the clothes are very ancient.

My flock is not large. About a dozen men, including two elderly brothers named Cheesehill who fancy themselves as art experts and are looking forward to the opportunity of pitting their wits against the gullible Frog stall-holders. The Gorringers are also coming, which makes me positively bubble with gloom.

Once again we take to the Metro, which the Gorringers are not happy about. We pile into a compartment, but they wish to be away from the maddening crowd and get into a carriage on their own.

We rattle along to the Porte de Clignancourt Station, where I open the doors and we step out. I shepherd my brood on the platform and wait for the Gorringers. I see them standing by the closed doors of their carriage, waiting for them to spring open, like on the Underground. Bad news time for the Gorringers. There is a catch – and you have to lift it yourself.

I am about to shout to them, when I get an unexpected Frog in my throat (like Linda Lovelace when she visited Paris) and the words somehow won't come. So, being terribly British and with their upper lips positively frozen stiff,

122

the Gorringers are carried away to an unknown destination.

Nobody sheds any tears at this French misconnection.

For the benefit of those not cognisant of the nature of the Paris flea market, I will read to you from the Rupert Colt handout on the subject, ignoring all the spelling and typing errors.

'The market is divided up into five parts. Vernais, which is mainly junk with dolls and clothes mixed with old furniture. This is the place to pick up a bargain. Malik, where there are records, shoes and very ancient clothes. This is the place for fleas. Biron for reasonable furniture. Jules Valles for books and musical instruments. Paul Bert for oddments and stuff brought in from demolition firms.'

There. Isn't that a load of useful information? When Jonathan May tells you something, you know it's true.

The Cheesehills can't wait, and as soon as we get into the market they're off like ferrets down a rabbit-hole, little noses sniffing the air for bargains. Out of interest, and as I've got to stay there to get them all back anyway, I follow them round at a discreet distance.

They pass a stall loaded with bric-à-brac, run by an old man who would have made Toulouse-Lautrec look like Joe Bugner. He is like a bundle of rags done up ugly. I swear I can see his clothes actually walking around on his skinny body.

George and Julian – the Cheesehills – glance about the stall and George suddenly freezes. He grabs Julian by the shoulder and hauls him into the shadows. They don't notice me.

'Julian. Did you see that picture?'

'Where?'

'There. Behind the bust of Beethoven. To the left of the pair of knockers.'

I perk up at that and peer about for the afore-mentioned boobs. All I can see is a pair of brass lions that look like . . . sorry, door knockers. Shouldn't have raised your hopes like that.

Julian peers into the gloom at the back of the stall and

123

immediately begins to shake. Greed starts to sweat out of his narrow, rat-like face, and his fingers begin to clutch and maul each other. It is the most sickening sight I have seen since I accidentally walked into the bathroom when my aunt Gloria was staying with us and she'd dropped the soap.

The picture they're talking about looks nothing to me.

'It's a genuine Nolan. Isn't it?'

'Yes, yes, it is. Look at the brushwork. Oooh, yes. Only Nolan could have painted an angel like that.'

It doesn't look much like an angel to me. More like a dissipated gunman; still, I suppose they know what they're talking about.

'That must be worth at least sixty thousand pounds.'

'Act casual, Julian. Let me handle it. That Frenchman mustn't guess what he's got there.'

They stroll to the stall, as casual as if they were going to be presented to the queen. The old man looks up vacantly as they approach. George points at a china bullfrog.

'How much is that, please?'

'In English money, monsieur, it is one pound.'

'Thank you, and that?' pointing this time at a copper bowl of such hideous design that I wouldn't even give it to my brother Morrie.

'Seventy-five pence, monsieur.'

So it goes on, with them asking the price of all the tat around. Nothing over two pounds.

'That barometer?'

'Alas. It is broken, monsieur. Only one pound seventy pence.'

Now, the moment has come. Unable to keep the note of strain from cracking in his voice, Julian points at *the* picture.

'That old painting in the corner. How much do you want for that?'

Both brothers are already hugging themselves with glee at the thought of the superb coup they're about to pull off.

'The picture of the angel, monsieur?'

'Yes, yes.'

'Seventy thousand pounds, monsieur.'

Collapse of skinny parties.

That night the whole party is booked in for supper at the 'Damp Pussy' night club. Hardly the Moulin Rouge for class, it has one outstanding virtue that attracts Rupert Colt to it.

It is very cheap.

There is hardly anyone else there when we arrive, and the place has all the charm of a cast-off corset. There are violet lights flickering around the ceiling in a failed attempt to give it glamour. The tables are small and shaky and the waitresses resemble the Russian street-sweepers I showed round Birmingham. If you can remember that far back. There is a gilded cage in the middle of the room where we are told the lovely go-go dancers will perform for our delectation.

They seem to have gone – gone at the moment. Which is worse than a can-can dancer who can't.

I slip off for a jimmy riddle and find the gents is as dark as a coyote's cupboard. I am about to aim Edgar at the earthenware, when a hand stops me in mid-jet.

'For the service, monsieur,' croaks a voice like old Minnie Bannister.

Service! It can't be a place of religion. Suddenly, the centime drops. I have seen movies where they have French loos. Each loo has an old loo-lady who gets a small gratuity for handing you the paper, or whatever.

I dig into my pocket and fork out a handful of loose change. Or, should it be loo's change?

Ho, ho, not to mention ho! Merriment and whatnot.

When I get back I find the meal is well under way. With some meat that is well underdone and a bill already there that is well over what was agreed. I query it with the manager, and he mutters something about a 'trois jours semaine', whatever that is. He finally knocks off ten per cent, and everyone tucks in.

They say French cooking can knock spots off all other

kinds. I wish it would knock the spots of mould off my fish. There is a fleeting moment when I wonder whether my mum has got a job at the Damp Pussy.

A group of ageing Sicilians arrive and begin to pluck out some modern pop music, beginning with 'The Little White Cloud That Cried' and moving on to 'Living Doll'. A light spits on over the gilded cage and some birds start to gyrate.

Most of them are the usual tired old tarts, but there is one who is not bad, in a florid sort of way. All of them are wearing fantastically thick make-up. I doubt I would even recognise my own sister Melanie if she were one of them.

The absurdity of the thought amuses me, and I get up to shake a leg with a hot potato from Rotherham. The evening is not going badly, and all thoughts of Rupert Colt are vanishing in a haze of alcohol. Miss Bootle from Rotherham is pressing her warm body against me, and trying to chew my left ear off.

The go-go dancers are still going-going, especially the blonde one who is really letting it all hang out. Watching her go-go makes me want to come-come.

I have my hands full with Miss Bootle, but I fancy the dancer. Miss Bootle comes over all odd with an excess of the imitation champagne and has to go and rest. I park myself at a table near the wall and sit down. To my amazement, the dancer waves at me.

Casually, I wave back, unable to believe my luck. I am actually being as modest as ever there, because you have this sort of thing happening all the time when you have my looks.

The number ends – it has a vague similarity to 'Garden of Eden' – and the girl opens the cage door and skips over to join me. There is something about her that I seem to recognise. Maybe it's the heavy make-up. It certainly isn't the clothes. Gold lamé bra. Gold lamé knickers. Gold lamé boots. Quite dazzling.

'Hello, love, let me get you a drink.'

That seems to surprise her, as though she'd expected me to say something else, but then she grins and nods her head. 'All right, cherie. I don't mind if I do.' The voice is husky and unmistakably French. Can't miss it.

The drinks come, and we sit looking at each other. Where have I seen her before. I shift my chair so we're sitting close together. I accidentally-on-purpose drop my hand and let it rest casually on her thigh.

'You like me, cherie?'

'Yes. Yes, I do.'

'You would like to come back to my place, cherie, and make the jig-a-jig?'

By the gold lamé! These French birds leave our cold English girls miles behind. I like an outspoken girl myself, but this is a bit much. Still, in for a centime, in for a franc. I mean, we are all in the same Market now. I shall extend my own entente cordiale.

'Yes. I would very much like to make the jig-a-jig with you, mademoiselle.'

'But it is against the law, you naughty old monsieur, you.'

'What do you mean? Against the law?'

Suddenly the husky French voice disappears, and she speaks in the nasal tones of the Black Country.

'Because I'm your bleeding sister, you dirty git.'

My sister Melanie. I said there was something familiar about her, didn't I? I thought she was about to break into the movies. Despite her objections and those of the owner of the Damp Pussy, I whisk her back to my hotel, making her wash off her make-up first. Otherwise, I doubt they would have let either of us in.

Safely in my room, with a cup of coffee in her hand, she is my little sister once again. Eyes as friendly as a trapped cobra. As trustworthy as a money-lender's handshake.

'You want to know what I'm doing there?'

'That is the general idea, yes.'

'Well, Morrie and I were together for a bit, but he's got a new business he's running. Something in the same line of business as yourself, you might say.'

'Why the Damp Pussy?'

'Well, it's run by this simply smashing Corsican gangster called "One Ear".'

'Why is he called . . . ?'

'Because he's only got one ear, of course. Incidentally, you shouldn't have told Henri where you were taking me. One Ear's very jealous and he'll think you're after me. He's very short-tempered.'

'Never mind that, Melanie. What about you becoming a star?'

'Oh, that.'

'Yes, that.'

'Well, all my plans were laid . . .'

'And you got laid instead.'

She grins at me. 'Jonny, you're getting better. That's dead right. One Ear took me away from this jazz musician who'd taken me away from this financier who'd taken me away from this gay dress designer who'd taken me away from this footballer from Manchester on holiday who'd taken me away from the film director.'

Listening to the sagas of Melanie's affairs is like those bits in the Bible where Simeon begat Saul and Saul begat Benjamin and Benjamin begat Cecil! You know.

'So what are you doing now?'

'Just doing my own thing, Jonny love. But what about you? You're in the travel business like Morrie.'

'Morrie's in the travel business?!'

She goes all defensive. 'Well, not exactly in the travel business. That sort of thing.'

I reckon that she might have told me more, but at that very moment there is a thunderous knocking at the door.

'Who on earth's that? Probably some drunk members of my tour party eager for a rebate.'

Melanie has risen to her feet, her face paler than usual. She puts her coffee down and looks round like my old man when the rent man cometh.

'It's probably One Ear, come to take me back to the club.'

'You're not going to be in the club while I'm around,' I say.

'I should hope not, brother. Incest is all very well, but not among your own family.'

The knocking gets louder and I hear a voice shouting. It

128

does not sound like an English voice. I wave Melanie into the bathroom and go to the door.

When I open it, my first thought is that a gorilla has escaped from the Rue Morgue Entertainments Centre and has happened on my door. Then I see that it is slightly more humanoid than a gorilla.

'You are the man who has taken my little flower?'

I strike my Englishman-abroad-dealing-with-the-foolish-natives pose. 'Look here, my good man . . .'

A fist as big as a side of beef lifts me off the floor by the collar. 'Where is she?'

I decide that it will be better to try and explain to him in short sentences that Melanie is really my sister and that it is all a dreadful misunderstanding. While he holds me there, I notice that he really does only have one ear.

'Now look here . . .'

I hear Melanie, shrieking from the doorway of the bathroom: 'Jonny, whatever you do don't call him . . .'

'One Ear, why don't you and . . .'

'. . . One Ear! He goes mad.'

He goes mad.

When I come round, they have both gone. I stagger into the bathroom to appraise the damage, which isn't as bad as it feels. There is a note on the mirror from Melanie.

'Sorry, Jonny. Must split. See you in London sometime. Your loving sister, Melanie.'

Not if I see her first. This makes my mind up. Rupert Colt is going to have a lot to answer for, when I get back to London the day after tomorrow.

Friday the thirteenth will not be a gay day for our Rupert.

CHAPTER TEN

You will all be interested to know what sort of fun I had on my last day in Paris. In the morning I spend all the time tracking down a dentist who will repair the minor damage to the structure of my teeth and jaw. The dentist I finally find asks me what I ran into.

'I think it was a left cross followed by two right jabs,' I reply wittily. He doesn't smile. Maybe it loses something in the translation.

It costs a lot of money but I am consoled by the thought that I can get it back from Rupert's collective insurance scheme. In the afternoon I wander across Paris to the local office of the said insurance company to collect the money back.

Much banging of foreheads and shrugging of shoulders. What a pity! It was only last week that they sent Monsieur Colt in London a notice that all cover had been suspended as he hadn't paid any premiums for six months. How unlucky!

Just one more little item in the rapidly expanding debit column against the name of Rupert Colt. When we get back to London tomorrow, I think I may have a look at the boot of the coach again.

The evening passes with all the gaiety and speed of a pauper's funeral. Nobody seems eager to get back to the green and sinking land of England on the morrow. Many of the boys from the Quaffers decide to catch up on their drinking, though I would have thought they'd overtaken it long ago.

One of the more elderly gentlemen among them distinguishes himself by performing the 'Zulu Warrior' dance, beloved of drunken rugby players and other mentally-retarded individuals. The dance culminates in the said bloke stripping off all of his clothes in the bar of our hotel and having beer poured all over him. This is great fun – they all think – but they will not think so in the morning when I pass on the management's bill for damages to carpets and furniture.

Just before we all troop off to our rooms – or, in the case of certain members, to each other's rooms – I make a little speech on behalf of the Company.

The usual guff about thanking them for their part in making the tour such a roaring success and hoping to see them back again next year. This moment, Rupert has told me, is when someone will call for a whip-round for the courier. Sure enough, a middle-aged gentleman's outfitter from Selly Oak clambers to his feet.

Mutters a few words about how they've all enjoyed it. There is a stony silence from everyone else, and even he seems to find his lies embarrassing. But he's coming to the bit about a whip-round. I have positioned myself near the only exit and all attempts to slink off to bed are met by a hearty smile and my shoulders blocking the doorway.

'Now we come to Jonny May. What can I say about him that we don't already know?' No answer. 'I think that we ...should...make...'

At this moment a glazed expression creeps slowly across his crêpy cheeks and he begins to slide gently down the wall. I have seen this sort of thing happen too often with my old man to have any hopes of a quick recovery. I rush to prop him up, slapping his face and muttering desperate endearments in his ears.

All to no avail. He begins to snore and rolls over on his side. I turn to the others to get them to help me get him up to his room.

Nothing. And nobody. The rotten crew have slunk off and left me with the baby. All seventeen stone of him.

By the time I've struggled upstairs with him and dumped him on his bed, there isn't a sign of anyone still up, though the hotel corridors resound to giggles and the padding of bare feet until early morning.

There is a brief interruption when Miss Bootle from Rotherham knocks on my door at four-fifteen, all giggly and in a state of undress. I reckon that this may be a lucky night after all and invite her in.

She sits on the bed, legs apart, hiccupping. 'I had to come and say good-bye to you, Jonny. And let you have a little something to remember me by.'

If the rest of her is anything to go by, the little something will be not unlike a drive through the Mersey Tunnel in a bubble car.

Still, never look a gift horse in the mouth. A bird in the bed is worth a bookful of telephone numbers. Just as I am about to ask her to join me, she grins up at me.

'I hope you're my lucky number tonight. Some of my earlier numbers weren't very good. But they were a bit tiddley.'

What does she mean? Can it be there have been a couple of others through the pink portal before me? I don't fancy that idea at all. How many? I wonder.

'Yes,' she giggles. 'Thirteen. Lucky for some.'

Not me, sweetheart. Her size nines don't even hit the carpet on the way out.

And a bonne nuit to you too!

We arrive back at Dover. The white cliffs gleam in the morning sunshine and there is a lump in my throat. I realise I have tied my tie too tight and loosen it.

The Customs man asks me if I have anything to declare.

'Yes. A black eye, two loose teeth, an upset stomach and an empty wallet.'

He is not amused. In fact, he spends the next ten minutes going through my suitcase which contains a rich and varied assortment of dirty clothes. It is only then that he scribbles the cryptic sign on my case and I am through.

One of the Swillers is alongside me. When the chalk mark goes on his suitcase, he turns to me with a grin and says: "Does that mean I've won?"

The Customs men are really good sports. They take him off into a side room and he has still not reappeared when we depart on the coach bound for London.

Gradually, people get off, swearing to write and not to lose touch. You know the sort of thing. Everyone says it and nobody does it!

At last, we are in central London, and we can bid a fond farewell to each other. Hugh manipulates the coach round Soho, so I can call in on Rupert and collect the bread he owes me, then we can drive off together to Caledonian Road and our little grey home in the north.

The office is closed. Not only is it closed, but it looks as though it is likely to remain closed. I once saw some pictures of the tomb of Tutankhamen – the old Egyptian mummy – and it was like a dark cave, filled with dust. This is exactly what the head office of Colt Enterprises looks like.

There is mail piled up on the floor inside under the letter-box, and it looks as though nobody's been here for weeks. Stuck inside the window is a faded scrap of paper, with a message typed on it. It says: 'Weregret that Clot Entrepirse hasmoved to another addressss$\frac{1}{2}$. FurtherenXenuqiries to Mrscravta at cake shop at 435.'

From the typing I guess that Rupert himself has done it. I suss out that he means Mrs. Cravat at Number Forty-three and toddle along.

At first she denies all knowledge of Rupert Colt, saying she's fed up to the teeth with people coming and wasting her time. She doesn't know where he's gone or anything about him. Then she peers at me.

'Wait a minute. You used to work for him, didn't you?'

That 'used to' sends a cold shiver through my bank balance. I nod my head. 'I'm May.'

Fortunately she is too flustered with muttering customers waiting to be served to make the usual joke and rummages under the counter, coming up with a tatty and crumpled envelope. It is marked: 'Jonathanmay.,;. tTo be callled for!?.'

My fingers trembling, I hop out and climb in the coach, where Hugh is having little success in chatting up a traffic warden, who would not be out of place in 'Bride of Frankenstein Has Risen From the Grave – Yet Again!'

We set off for Holloway with Hugh trying to turn round and see what's in the letter *and* drive. I open the letter.

It is hand-written in lilac ink. There is no date and no address. 'Dearest Jonny, I am sorry that things have not really worked out. One or two problems have come up, and I think it will be better for my health if I toddle off to a sunnier clime for the next few months. You will, I know, be worried about your remuneration. I have all too little myself. So I have made the following arrangements with a man who is, shall we say, my sleeping partner. Not in the way that you might think, though, duckie. Tell Thomas to take the coach to the usual place and then leave it. My partner will come along tonight and pick up one or two things and will then pay both Thomas and yourself. I am sorry about this, but I hope it doesn't change your plans about being a courier. It is a strangely rewarding occupation with more than its fair share of surprises.'

He can say that again. Thomas is keeping up a running commentary on Rupert's background and failings that must be burning the little man's ears, wherever he is.

There is a P.S. to the letter. 'I am sure that both Hugh and yourself must be feeling down in the dumps at this awful news. Perhaps I can cheer you with a little story that may bring back a smile to your faces. It seems there were two gay young men who found themselves locked out of their dwelling late at night. So they scout around and find a ladder, ready to climb in through an open window. Sandy agrees to go up the ladder, while his friend holds it still. Halfway up he stops. "Rollo!" he hisses down to his chum. "I feel just like a fireman." "Don't be silly, Sandy," says Rollo. "Where would you find one at this time of night?" All for now. Your adoring friend, Rupert Colt.'

So, that's it. So much for my ambitions and for making it on the millionaires' circuit. So much for being able to laugh at my obnoxious brother Morrie (short for Morello, in case you'd forgotten. My mum was crazy about that cherry jam when she was carrying him.) I fear I shall never have the chance to laugh at Morrie. He always ends one up on me.

At last we get back to Bacon Hill. To rub salt into my wounds, there is another note waiting there from the lovely Linda Loveband. She has gone on a week's holiday with a friend and will I look after her dog? Edgar droops to unprecedented lengths. He sinks so low that I fear he might never rise again.

Hugh is determined to go out and get drunk that night to wash away his despair at the collapse of Colt Enterprises, and urges me to join him.

There is the germ of an idea burrowing away in my mind and I refuse. I can see a way I can get back at the untrustworthy Mr Colt and maybe make a little for myself on the side. Thomas is so distraught that I have no trouble in getting him to accept my kind offer to drive the coach down to this mysterious garage for him.

I know I don't have a licence for that sort of vehicle! Why quibble about little details like that when the climax is near? If there's one thing I hate it's having my climaxes ruined by a little quibble at the last minute.

In some ways I reckon that I ought to be sitting in my flat, feeling like a spare bric-à-brac at a flea market wedding. But the fighting blood of the Mays is roused. I intend to beard this mysterious Mr Big in his den. Providing he's not too Big. I will demand a good deal, or I will spill the Heinz to the fuzz. Note how I slip easily into the parlance of the Underworld.

Hugh James David Thomas has given me explicit instructions on how to get to the garage and exactly what to do when I get there. 'Whatever happens, don't touch anything or take anything out of the coach,' he says. 'Just leave it as it is and the man will pick up what he's got to pick up.'

He is more cagey than Dudley Zoo about what is in the coach. I don't let on that I've got a good idea where it's hidden. He roars off into the night on his moped, and I get ready for Operation Get Jonny's Money Back.

Stage one is accomplished easily enough. I have never driven anything quite as big as the coach before, but the power-assisted steering makes it a fairly easy task. Apart from a small scratch along one side where I didn't *quite* judge the width.

I find the garage near Highbury and drive round the back. There is a huge antiquated padlock on the door and the inside is as inviting as a dromedary's den. I back the coach in, and shut the door.

The garage is on two levels. The higher level is where I've come in, and it is like a big, high balcony above the front of the building. I suppose there's a drop of about twenty feet to the floor. It's crowded with the coach shut away, and I worry a bit about unloading the loot – whatever it is – on such a narrow space.

Just to get the feel of the layout, I climb down the shaky ladder and shuffle through thick oil to the front door. I can dimly hear the rumble of heavy traffic. I reckon that this is where Mr Big will come in. The back way in is very dirty and tatty. Not the sort of thing for a boss of international crime.

Directly under the balcony, I nearly terminate this story a few pages earlier. There is a creaking from the floor. I hop away as lightly as Nureyev and wonder whether there is a booby-trap left for the unwary.

No; it is some kind of inspection pit with a cracked cover. I lever the edge up and peer into the noisome depths. It looks as deep and inviting as the Black Hole of Calcutta and smells like my mum's Irish stew.

I carefully tip back the cover and return to the rear of the coach. Now, this is the moment of truth. Will I find a cache of goodies, or will I find nothing and look the biggest charlie since that bloke strapped on wings and tried to fly off the Eiffel Tower? He wanted to make an impression, he said. He did – four foot deep in the road!

The boot tips back and I peer into the musty interior. As far as I can see, it's empty. I have borrowed a torch from the adorable Miss Loveband and I flash it around. I like a good flash every now and again, don't you? Tones up the muscles.

Yes! No! Yes, there it is! A small sort of handle set flush with the side of the boot. I drag it open and there are several parcels inside.

What will it be? Gold? Drugs? (I hope not. If it is, I shall for once put away my financial interests and tip them in the sludge pit.) Paintings?

They are bleeding heavy, I can tell you that.

The first parcel is rectangular and about eighteen inches high. With my trusty penknife – well, you never know when you're going to have to dig a boy scout out of a horse's hoof – I slit open the top edge.

This is obviously the Dutch parcel. There is 'Hot Licks' from Amsterdam, as well as 'Gobble', 'Yum' and other assorted hard-core magazines. I reckon, from my casual expeditions round Soho, that this lot could sell for a fiver each. And, there's about a hundred here. Plus one other parcel. All hard-core. Plus an apple-core, which I throw away.

Two leather cases reveal some lovely small pieces of Italian crystal. Smashing pieces. Very erotic figurines and shapes, all mixed up together.

I put them on top of the mags.

Next out of the hat – well, boot then – is a flattish box that I can hear ticking. I've heard of businesses doing a bomb, but this is ridiculous. I open it gingerly and there are row upon row of best Swiss timepieces. No cuckoo clocks though.

That's Amsterdam, Rome and Zurich done for. What about Paris? Now I know why the route of the tour was so odd. Rupert and his boss obviously sent their coach wherever they knew there was illicit merchandise to be lifted. Straight through Customs and no questions.

The Paris goodies are in a soft bag, with three boxes inside. They chink slightly as I open them. Chinoiserie? No. Super-expensive perfume all with names like Bicci and Rocci and Guggi. I have a whiff and it nearly knocks my hat off. I suppose that's a sign it's good.

I pile them on top of all the other stuff, noting with some concern that the heap of contraband rocks a bit. I steady it with a careful hand. It wouldn't do to have my salary and a bit of profit on the side going down in a jingling, ticking, smelling heap.

Then I sit back and wait. It won't be dark for another couple of hours and I doubt that the boss will arrive before then. There is a small light by the courier's seat in the coach and I settle down to read.

Fortunately, I have come prepared. I cheer myself up by reading for the eleventh time my well-thumbed copy of *Confessions of a Shop Assistant* by a young author of immense talent. If you haven't read it, you really ought to. A laugh a minute; if you read fast!

Time passes so quickly that I've only just got to the bit where you-know-who comes in to buy her knickers and I hear a creaking somewhere near the front. I dim the glim and walk as quietly as I can to the edge of the balcony, feeling my way in the blackness. My hand brushes the top of the smuggled goods and I stop. Another step and I will be in the air. Not for long though. The sludge pit is only twenty feet down!

I hear feet walking outside. A key grating in the lock. A dim figure against the light of the street lamps. The door closing. Careful steps through the slippery oil and then the click of a light switch.

Because of the height I'm at I can't see the person who comes in right away. There is a smart snap-brim hat, and I can see the shoulders of a very expensive-looking overcoat. The flash of a diamond tie-pin. The sheen of well-polished leather shoes.

I reckon it might give him a nasty shock if I let him climb up the ladder and then discover he's not as alone as he thinks. I wait till he's right underneath me, on the edge of the sludge pit, and I cough.

'Good evening!'

He leaps back as though he's found a wasp in his jock-strap and stares up at me. The light shines full on his face. It is white with shock.

Not as white as mine when I see that face.

This is a fright break for you to gather breath ready for the last stumbling revelation.

I don't care if you do know who it is! You'll sit back and take your fright break like everyone else.

Nearly over.
Right.

The shock as I see the face of Mr Big is so intense that I fall backwards. I feel the pile of stuff wobble and I try and grab at it.

Too late.

I give a strangled groan as my feet slip from under me and I topple base over apex. The man below gives an unstrangled scream as he sees a pile of boxes and parcels begin to fall towards him. He must think it's an assassination attempt by another gang.

I hear a sticky thud, which I guess is him falling flat on his face in the inches of filth around the garage.

I hear an expensive-sounding tinkle as the first box smashes on the inspection lid of the pit. For a moment the garage fills with the fumes of a lot of bottles of costly perfume all breaking at once.

The glass goes next, in a misty crystal glitter, smack on top of the perfume. I get to my feet and reach out a despairing hand for the watches, only to have them slip through my fingers.

Time flies.

Crash. Time stops.

The pile of porn is still as high as an elephant's eye, and I lean on it to look over the top. I hear weeping.

Mr Big now looks rather little, and has crawled on his hands and knees to where the mangled remnants of his hoard lie in a silent, splintered, stinking mess.

'God! What have I done to deserve this? Who is that enemy up there? I will tear his head from his body. I will . . .'

Suddenly, I am fed up with the whole thing. Money may be important, but not that much. Feeling thoroughly choked-off with travel couriering and all it entails, I give the bottom pile of porny mags a resounding kick with my cuban-heel boots. It relieves my feelings.

That is not all it does. It disturbs their centre of gravity.

I have just time to bellow a warning to the grovelling figure below when the lot whistles down, on top of the refuse of the other parcels, and clean through the broken cover of the oil pit.

On holiday once, my old man fell asleep on a chemical toilet, and got stuck. We had to heave him off it, and when he came free there was this unforgettable sucking noise. The sound made by the smuggled goods plopping into several feet of old sludge is not dissimilar. A wave of oil shoots as high as the balcony, before splattering back to the floor.

I risk another look over the edge. Mr Big has now become Mr Dirty. He is covered in oil. There is no sign of any of the loot, just the tank of blackness, bubbling and chuckling quietly to itself. The grease and slime has soaked everything for yards around.

A face turns up and glares at me. If looks could kill, Jonny would be plucking on his harp by now.

(Publisher's Note: Or stoking the fires!)

It is an odd face. The hair is plastered thickly to the skull. The face is shiny black with oil. The lips stand out like a red cupid's bow and the eyes are two rolling billiard balls, flecked with red.

My moment has come.

I shout down: 'Hello, Morrie. Why don't you give us a chorus of "Swanee River"?'

And I begin to laugh. And laugh and laugh.

I waited a long time to get a chance to laugh down at my brother Morrie, or Mr Big as he was once known. It's worth all that lost money *and* the lost job.

Linda is back from her holiday and we lie comfortably in bed, while Edgar licks his lips – well, somebody's lips – like a cat who's just had his cream. Which he has.

She is highly amused by my stories, which I edit slightly to avoid any mutual embarrassment. There is a wind on the heath. Life is sweet, brother. That old poet knew what he was on about.

In the morning I'll go off down the Labour and see what they can offer me this time.

But that, as they always say in books, is another story.

And it will be.

A Selection of General Fiction from Sphere

Some new books in the CONAN series from Sphere.
CONAN was created by one of the greatest science fantasy
writers, Robert E. Howard. The collections of short stories
were first published in 'Weird Tales' in the 1930's and
CONAN is Howard's only full-length novel. The stories are
edited by the distinguished science fiction writer L. Sprague
de Camp.

All Sphere Books are available at your bookshop or
newsagent, or can be ordered from the following address:

Sphere Books, Cash Sales Department,
P.O. Box 11, Falmouth, Cornwall.

Please send cheque or postal order (no currency), and allow
7p per copy to cover the cost of postage and packing
in U.K. or overseas.